I0526629

# BREACHED

## MYSTIC ASSASSIN SERIES

## T. L. CRATER

Crystal Star Publishing
1303 Alexandria St.
Lafayette, CO 80026
https://crystalstarpublishing.com

*Breached*
A Novella in the Mystic Assassin Series

by T.L. Crater

Cover art by FrinaArt
Editing by Jeff DeMarco

Copyright 2021 T.L. Crater

Printed in the United States of America
Worldwide Electronic & Digital Rights
1st North American and UK Print Rights

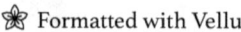 Formatted with Vellum

# CONTENTS

# 1

Rainey threw her gym bag over her shoulder and headed for the door of the Boston Women's Martial Arts dojo. "Thanks for inviting me," she said to the young woman walking beside her.

"Oh, my Goddess. Thank you for coming. I can't believe you agreed to do it. You're so talented. I had no idea when I saw you doing forms in the park how much you knew." Jessica put her hand over her mouth, her face flushing red, apparently realizing she'd been gushing.

Rainey gave her an easy smile. "It was my pleasure. I love sharing tips, especially with advanced students."

"You really taught us a lot. Can I get you to come back? I didn't even get your phone number." Jessica pushed a strand of sweat-drenched hair behind her ear.

Coming here, teaching in public, was a big risk, but one Rainey was willing to take. Her contract work for a private security group required anonymity. Complete secrecy, in fact. Her own parents thought she was dead. But teaching women to defend themselves was a passion for her.

"I'm not sure how much longer I'll be in town," Rainey said, "but if it turns out I have the time, I'll drop by and see if you've got an opening."

"We'll make time for you."

Then Rainey spotted him. The man in a brown trilby hat sitting on a bench at the bus stop a block up the street. It looked like Control had a job for her. Rainey squeezed Jessica's shoulder and said, "Gotta run."

Jessica gave her a little wave, then turned back into the lobby. Rainey strolled toward the sidewalk until the young woman disappeared into the dojo, then hurried off. Control's courier caught her eye. He raised his hat and resettled it on his head, their signal, then walked away toward a coffee shop across the street.

Rainey reached the bus stop quickly and took a seat on the bench where the man had been. She leaned back, pretending to be winded. A bus lumbered to a stop and opened its doors with a wheeze. In the bustle of passengers disembarking and others getting on, she leaned down and detached a small envelope beneath the bench.

The weight surprised her. Usually these packages had a thumb drive inside, but she felt a solid rectangular object in this one. Probably one of 7R4C3R's specialty items. Rainey hadn't realized how to pronounce this strange pseudonym until she'd heard Control call his hacker 'Tracer.' She'd never met him in person.

Rainey made her way down a side street in the cooling summer evening, watching for any tails. Seeing nothing, she hit the fob to unlock her used Prius and slid behind the wheel. Placing the envelope in the passenger seat, she pulled into the light traffic and drove the short distance to her apartment in Lower Alston, taking a few false turns along the way. Nobody was following her. Not unless they'd put a team on her that handed her off to each other from time to time.

Rainey always moved to a new town after an assignment. This time she'd picked Boston. University neighborhoods worked best. The undergrads clustered in Alston and the neighborhood was more international, but she hadn't been able to resist the Charles River Reservation. It was the perfect place to run and do her Kajukenbo forms. Nobody gave her a second look. Except Jessica, who'd been going through her own routine early one morning. But Jessica and her organization had checked out. Very low risk.

She maneuvered her Prius into a spot in the street behind her apartment and walked down the sidewalk, swinging her gym bag to appear casual as she scanned the area. Large-leafed sycamores shaded the street, creating shadows for her to move through. The sidewalks were empty, so she slipped into the alley that ran through to her building, walked to the front, and pushed open the door.

The small lobby was empty. A bank of old mailboxes filled one side. A dusty plastic flower arrangement sat in front of a gilded mirror opposite them. Discarded ads littered the table beside the vase. Relieved not to run into any neighbors, she took the steps two at a time to the third floor and then strolled down the hallway to the end to her corner apartment.

The transparent tape at the top of her door was undisturbed. Inside, Rainey did a quick security sweep and found everything as she'd left it. She checked the street below, looking for any unfamiliar cars, but found nothing new. Satisfied, she threw her gym bag into the bedroom and walked into the kitchen, where she placed the envelope onto the small table.

Rainey always observed the same ritual when listening to a possible assignment. She knew it might be the last quiet time she'd have for a while. She put on the kettle and took out the latest cast iron teapot she'd found in Boomerangs, a thrift shop in Central Square. The type of tea depended on the time of day, so for this evening she chose chamomile. She sprinkled in some rose petals and tossed in a vanilla bean. She picked a blue mug large enough for soup, added a dab of blueberry honey, and waited.

The kettle whistled and she poured water into the pot, leaning over to enjoy the first burst of rose scent. She put the lid on and opened the envelope. Inside was a phone. She switched it on, touched her thumb to the home button, and it unlocked.

*Control must have my fingerprints on file somewhere,* she thought.

Not unexpected, but still, she didn't like how much they knew about her.

There was one number stored in the phone's memory.

Before clicking on the entry, she poured tea and took a sip, closing her eyes to savor the unique combination of flavors.

Then she made the call.

"I have a mission, should you choose to accept it," Control said in his well-modulated voice. There was no hint of sarcasm.

Rainey chuckled at his old TV show reference. He always used it. "To what do I owe the pleasure of an actual phone call?"

"It's nice to talk to you as well," he said, pretending offense.

She took another sip of tea and waited.

"Our friends in the agencies need help. They're overwhelmed with leads from the recent coup attempt."

"I can imagine."

Many people who stormed the capitol after the election had been ordinary citizens who'd gone down the rabbit hole of conspiracy theories, following the trail left by bloggers known by single letters and tweets from politicians. Not to mention so-called news channels. These people imagined themselves to be saving their country from corruption. Some claimed late President Earl had been assassinated to clear the way for his challenger to win. Some blamed the opposition party. Others foreign actors.

Only Rainey and the girl she'd rescued from his bedroom knew the truth. She hadn't been forced to use the syringe she'd brought to simulate a natural death. President Earl had died from a heart attack without any assistance from her.

Besides misguided citizens believing in improbable scenarios, who in the group was not hoodwinked? Who was still set on replacing the duly elected officials with their own group of candidates? And how clean was that slate? Earl had been a straight-up Russian asset. No question about it in her mind, although the conspiracy crowd would deny it to the end.

Earl had spouted about a rigged election for months before voting began last November. A number of domestic terrorist groups had coordinated the rebellion after the election, which had been months in the planning. Hell, they'd even printed t-shirts. Members of various law enforcement agencies and the military also participated. The question was in what capacity. It was a lot to sort out.

One thing was clear. It was unlikely everyone had packed up their Winchesters and gone home. What were their future plans? The agencies with their assorted alphabetical acronyms had been weakened by Earl, who'd replaced actual professionals with his cronies. The U.S. defense agencies were overwhelmed, plain and simple.

All this would be enough, but hackers had broken into government computers—agencies responsible for U.S. security, foreign and domestic. They'd left a mess. Files were stolen, corrupted, false information left behind. It was still being sorted out. The hack had made the news, but the FBI had been able to hide how serious the breach was.

"They said we need all hands on deck," Control said.

Rainey snorted. "Are we talking about the military here?"

"A mix, so some."

"Are you sure they didn't say every swinging . . . ?" She left the rest unsaid.

Control chuckled. "All right, they did, but—"

"Then that leaves me out," Rainey said. She took another sip of tea and tried to get comfortable in the vinyl kitchen chair.

"Please, Rainey. We need you. This conspiracy is extensive and, as it turns out, quite complicated."

"But this is not my specialty. I'm not an investigator. Find me a target and I'll go after it."

"You've been trained in all areas of spy craft, my dear."

Rainey bristled at the endearment. "But—"

"You're way better than you think. We know they've got more actions planned. We have to find out how the main actors are connected."

Rainey studied a slight bruise on her hand. Must have been from the training she'd just given.

"We've got to find out how deep this goes," Control said.

She could imagine him straightening his perfectly groomed hair, which is what he did when he was frustrated. She'd picked up a few of his tells. "Like I said, find me a target."

"Your country needs you," Control said in his low, cultured voice.

Damn the psychologists. They knew her trigger points.

Rainey shook her head in frustration. She'd just settled into her new neighborhood. Just found the perfect teapot. Now she'd have to move again. "What's the mission?"

"7R4C3R will upload it in thirty seconds. Please let me know by tomorrow at noon."

"That's fast," she said. She usually got three days to consult with her spiritual advisors if the target's name was not on her list of approved hits.

"Like I said, the situation is urgent."

Rainey started to end the call, but realized the line was still open. "I can't thank you enough," Control said. "I lost a friend in that attack."

"I'm sorry," she said.

"I'm a professional, but this—this is personal."

He ended the call before she could offer condolences. Control hated sentiment.

Rainey took a sip of her tea, but it was cold. She decided to make a fresh pot. She thought about what Jessica had shared. So many women had similar stories. After the gang rape in Afghanistan, Rainey's time at the Tibetan nunnery had done a lot to heal her trauma. Rising early, chanting with a group of women, some innocent, some also victims of violence, had brought her a peace she had not known existed in this life.

Rainey had almost died in Afghanistan. Four men led by the unit commander Brad Rogers had kidnapped her, taken her out into the desert, staked her out and raped her. One man after another. They choked her, beat her, burned her legs and sides with the muzzles of smoking gun barrels.

In point of fact, they had killed her. She remembered the relief as she flew out of her battered body while a man rutted on top of her, his hands wrapped around her neck, squeezing.

She sailed into a tunnel of light. Light that healed all it touched. Light that was all-encompassing love. Balm. Joy beyond words. The anguish, the fear and rage—it was all gone in an instant.

But before she made it through to the place she wanted to go with every fiber of her being, radiant forms of light barred the way. They handed her a scroll. She'd known what they were asking without any words being exchanged. Remove these people from their current life and send them to us.

For a split second, if there was any time there at all, Rainey wondered why they got to go into this glory and she didn't. But as soon as her glowing fingers closed around the scroll held out to her, she returned with a whoosh and woke in a local hospital with ER workers shouting over her body.

One thing was for sure. Madison Danika Varma was dead. She'd shed her old name and become Rainey.

She finished her second pot of tea and washed out the mug. Then she cleaned the teapot and dried it carefully. She'd take the assignment, but she wasn't going to leave this pot behind. She was tired of having to find new ones every time she moved. She'd ship it to Arnold. After the mission, she would travel to The Oaks. Mull over their last adventure in Peru and what it all meant. Right now, she had a country to save.

# 2

Rainey presented her fake employee badge to the scanner at the entrance to the FBI headquarters and prayed to whoever was on the spiritual roster to watch over her today that it would pass scrutiny. The light beeped green and she proceeded to the metal detector. She placed her messenger bag in the little bucket, fished out the keys to the car she'd been issued—a gas-guzzling Ford of some kind that handled like a tank—and walked through. The plastic components of the gun she carried, some in separate pockets and some stowed in her bag, did not disturb the machine.

She'd gotten new glasses in the D.C. arms depot from the Gadget Master—not his official title, that would be the Quartermaster, but she loved to tease him. He wore his hair pulled back in a ponytail, thin and scraggly, combed around the bald spot on top of his head. But his large, muscled shoulders and compact hips did not belong to a geek who'd spent his career inventing thingamajigs in a lab. He'd been in the field, of that she was certain. Which was why she called him the Gadget Master.

The glasses he'd designed sent data to the face recognition software in security cameras to keep her from being properly identified.

The frames were large and orange. A small camera was embedded in one of the endpieces.

"These will draw too much attention," she'd complained.

"Nah, they're all the rage these days," he'd said, "and they'll help camouflage your face."

Apparently not well enough. Now she had caught the attention of a guard, who waved her over.

"Random check. Your turn today." His voice was raspy, but didn't betray a lot of suspicion.

"No problem."

"Working the late shift?"

"I'm not sure if they'll let me go home in the morning," she replied, trying to share some employee grousing.

The man grunted and pointed to a pad with the outline of feet. Rainey assumed the position, a line of sweat breaking out on her upper lip. She hoped the man didn't get too thorough in the upper thigh area. He kept his frisk professional, stepped back and gestured for her to continue on her way.

She picked up her messenger bag from the conveyor belt and moved to the elevators. The earpiece just inside her ear canal gave an almost imperceptible chirp. 7R4C3R had turned off all the electronics while she was at security, in case they were monitoring signals.

The hacker's voice whispered in her ear. "I see you got through. Did they wand you?"

Rainey felt a surge of annoyance. She couldn't answer in the middle of a crowded elevator. The car emptied out on the next two floors. When the doors closed again and the elevator started to lift, she finally answered, "No wand."

"Great. So the badge worked."

"Uh-huh."

"Get off on the next floor and head to the ladies' room."

Rainey glanced up at the display. The car was moving too fast for the next level, so she pushed the button for a few floors up. It came to a stop quickly, leaving Rainey's stomach in her throat. She pulled on the bottom of her jacket to straighten it. Squared her shoulders. The doors swooshed open, and she stepped out into the hallway.

*I belong here,* she told herself.

An empty hallway stretched in front of her, each white door identical to the next. No signage indicated whether it opened to an office, a closet, or a lab.

"You skipped a couple of floors," he complained.

"Uh-huh."

"Let me catch up—Ah, fifth door on your right."

Rainey turned the knob and was relieved that it opened to a restroom. Nobody stood at the sinks. All the stall doors were open. She went into one and pulled a cell phone out. Switched it on and watched it load. A perfect hiding spot, considering she didn't know when she might get a chance to *go* after the mission was complete. She flushed the toilet, pulled up her pin-striped, polyester pants— god, she hated them—and went to the sink to wash up.

"Go back out and walk past the elevators, turn the corner, and go to the next door."

"OK," she said just as the door opened.

A blocky brunette walking in did a double take.

Rainey looked at the phone and pretended to end the call, then stuffed it into her pocket.

The woman nodded and went into a stall.

Rainey made her escape. The security cameras kept her company as she strolled along. She turned the corner and reached out to grasp the knob, but found a keypad instead.

In her ear, 7R4C3R called out a series of numbers. When she entered the last one, the light switched from red to green. The door opened to a custodial closet. Rainey snorted, "So they lock up the brooms, too?"

7R4C3R chuckled. "Some of these chemicals mix to pretty obnoxious solutions. They could be used as weapons."

"I'm in."

"You know the drill. Put on the fingerprint film and get comfortable. We'll let you know when shift change goes into high gear."

Rainey found a step stool to sit on and settled down to wait. She found herself thinking about her communiques with 7R4C3R. They'd worked together for two years, but their connection had been through texts, emails, and a one-off phone conversation. Only once, days ago, had they met face-to-face.

"Why is all this necessary?" Rainey had asked, looking around his office. She supposed it was his office.

They sat around a table holding a few mugs in the middle of a narrow room filled floor to ceiling with electrical equipment. Silver boxes of different sizes filled shelves on one side, all blinking green and blue lights merrily. Above them, various cords were curled up and hung on the wall. Opposite this sat a bank of computer monitors at the moment displaying a screen saver that showed a video of a whale breeching, then plunging into the water again, its enormous tail the last to submerge. It was calming, the detail pulling her eyes.

She made herself look back at 7R4C3R. "You used to just break into FBI files in a few minutes. It's nice to meet you, by the way."

"Likewise."

She studied the two men in front of her. The older one had a head of loose black curls and dark stubble on his cheeks. His brown eyes shone with avid intelligence. He was probably in his early thirties. So this was 7R4C3R.

"*Used to* is right. The Russian hack is ongoing and things are still a mess. Some of my programs got corrupted, so we're going to have to go old school. Hands on."

"I'm no expert."

"You don't need to be." He jumped up, retrieved something up off a shelf, then settled back in his chair. "The agencies have upped their security measures. Even hired some of my colleagues, so I just can't go marching in there. I might be recognized."

"One of your compatriots can't do this?"

"Unfortunately, no. You're our best option."

"Who am I impersonating?"

7R4C3R moved his mouse around and a woman's face appeared

on the laptop open on the table they were gathered around. "Shanice Greene. She's a supervisor on the swing shift."

A light-skinned African American woman with loose curls framing her face looked out at her. She wore large-framed glasses.

"Picks up a venti latte at her neighborhood Starbucks before taking the metro into work. We'll spike her drink so she'll call in sick."

"So, I just look like her?"

"Yes, but nobody will notice. She has a collection of bright big-framed glasses, so we'll get you some to match. Nemo here is too young for the job."

She looked up at the new recruit. So that's how you pronounced it. Control's emails referred to the new guy as N3M0.

The young man squirmed under her scrutiny. He pulled his black hoodie over his head in a vain attempt to stay hidden. Strands of blond hair escaped. He was too young for a beard. Rainey stopped herself from asking how old he was. She guessed around fourteen. Was it even legal to employ him?

"His specialty is—" 7R4C3R searched for a word "—digital forensics."

N3M0 shot him a disgusted look, which confirmed to Rainey they'd dumbed it down for her.

She interrupted before they geeked out. "By the way, 7R4C3R is a great acronym, but now that we've met . . ."

He studied her a moment, then pushed a stray lock out of his eyes. "You can call me Drake."

"Drake?" She knew better than to ask if that was his real name. "Better than that jumble of letters and numbers."

He nodded.

"What do you need me to do?"

Drake pushed a thumb drive across the table. She picked it up. The drive seemed to be encased in heavy metal, maybe titanium, and was a bit thicker than your average data stick. "Like I said, old school."

Now sitting in the cleaning supply closet at the FBI, a buzz in

Rainey's ear bud brought her back to the present. "Got the finger-prints on?" Drake asked.

Rainey took out the thumb drive containing the worm and stuck it into her underwire bra. She hated the bra, too, but Drake had said it would help camouflage the data stick. Next, she took out the silicon sheet that held the fingerprints of Rob Schmidt, one of the supervisors of the servers. They couldn't use Shanice Greene's since she was home sick. She just hoped she didn't set off any alarms.

Rainey peeled each silicon piece off and attached it to her fingertips, pressing each one long enough to allow her body to heat up the adhesive. After she attached the last one on her left pinky, Rainey held her hands out, fingers spread, for the requisite two minutes.

The sound of doors opening and muted conversations in the hallway reached her. She flexed her fingers. The film held fast. She took out the thick phone and glanced at the time. Five on the dot. These folks kept regular hours. That surprised her for some reason. She had no idea what they did on this floor, but they weren't the teams who measured their work hours by the mission rather than the clock.

She tried to hear their banter, hoping to glean something about them, but the walls were thick. After five minutes, the chatter died down to only the occasional voice. She'd wait two more minutes.

Drake's voice sounded in her ear. "We're ready. Go back to the elevator."

A glance at the time told her it had only been five minutes. "Another five minutes. Let them clear out."

"Not the plan. We want you to blend with the crowd. Take the elevator to the lobby."

Rainey stood and put her ear to the door. Hearing no sound in the hallway, she cracked the door open. Seeing nobody, she eased her way out into the empty corridor. Around the corner, three people walked together and another two waited by the elevator. She stopped to adjust her messenger bag.

"Keep going. We want you to blend in."

*I belong here,* she told herself again.

She followed at the same pace of the people in front of her. The elevator doors whisked open just as she arrived and everyone piled in, most checking their phones or relaxing against the walls with their eyes half closed, paying her no mind. Rainey did the same.

"These long days are killing me," one woman said to her in an undertone.

Rainey nodded. "That's the truth."

Before the woman could say more, the doors opened to the lobby, and they all joined the throng, headed for the parking lots and bus stops.

"Act like you forgot something," Drake reminded her.

Rainey let out an exasperated sigh, as much irritation that Drake thought she couldn't remember the plan as acting out her part, and stepped to the side. She searched through her bag.

"Walk to your left and around the corner."

There, she found two more elevators. One of them opened and disgorged people, these dressed in jeans and t-shirts. The elevator doors started to close.

"Get in."

Rainey jumped into the elevator. The doors slid shut, but the car didn't move.

"Take out the silver cylinder and click the end."

"I can remember instructions," Rainey grumbled under her breath.

She pressed the end of the cylinder and it extended. Inserted the tip into the key button and turned it left three times. The elevator moved down. After half a minute, the car bumped to a stop, and the doors opened to a crowd of people waiting to get on and go home. They parted for her to disembark.

"I worked forty-eight straight hours," a rangy man with longish hair said to a young woman as they walked by her.

"We're going to make mistakes if they don't stop pushing us so hard," she replied.

Rainey moved down the hall toward the double doors just past the group. Here was the most dangerous spot. She forced herself to breathe evenly. Rainey held her employee badge up to a scanner next to a glass door. After an interminable three seconds, the light switched from red to yellow. She walked into the security box.

The outer doors behind her locked with a loud click. The doors in front of her were also locked. She was trapped. If anything failed, she couldn't escape. A panel in the wall next to the inner door rose, presenting a keypad. She entered the sixteen-digit code, complete with capital letters, symbols, and numbers that Drake recited in her earpiece. How could anybody remember this? Thankfully, there were no hieroglyphs or Greek letters required.

The lock inside the inner steel door buzzed. Rainey pushed it open. Inside was a vestibule with a guard sitting behind bulletproof glass and an adjacent rack of slots marked 'cellphones.' *Damn*, each one of the slots had a lid marked with a number. No way she could see if anyone was already inside. Rainey slipped her cellphone into a slot, then walked to the bulletproof glass, surreptitiously angling her body away. The woman was busy talking to another security employee who was coming on for the next shift. She only glanced up.

Rainey splayed out her right hand on a panel next to the inner door and the machine read the fingerprints of Rob Schmidt. At least, she hoped it did. Her heart hammered in her chest.

*Just breathe,* she thought. *Smile and breathe.*

What would they do if they caught her? Couple decades in federal prison? Guantanamo Bay? *At least the weather is nice there,* she told herself. It wasn't like she was here to kill anyone. Just a little benevolent espionage.

After another eternity lasting about ten seconds, the light on the door to the server farm switched from yellow to green.

"And you're in," Drake said.

A wave of relief rushed through her and Rainey's clinched muscles released. She pushed the door open and walked inside.

*I belong here.* Rainey repeated her latest mantra a few times.

She walked toward the far wall that held a series of office cubicles. Banks of humming servers filled the SCIF, short for sensitive compartmented information facility. Small corridors ran between them, just big enough for human servants to administer to their electronic masters. Air-conditioning fans whirred in the ceiling in an almost successful attempt to keep the temperature down.

Before Rainey reached the back wall, Drake's voice instructed her to turn right. She checked around her, but most people were leaving or checking in for the evening, paying her no mind. She ducked down the cramped walkway and kept moving. In the relative privacy of the empty aisle, she reached for the thumb drive in her bra, making it look like she was scratching an itch in an embarrassing place. She found the drive and palmed it.

"Notice the labels on the shelves in the racks?" Drake didn't wait for a response. They'd gone over this earlier. "Look for MDF-02567."

Rainey slowed down and scanned the numbers on either side of her. A few racks down, she found it and stopped.

"OK," she mumbled.

"At the bottom, you'll see a row of USB ports. Put the thumb drive in the one two spaces from the right."

Rainey checked for people, but saw no one around her. The security cameras would record her, but once Drake had access, he could get in and delete the footage. He had explained that an external storage device would be flagged immediately, but it wouldn't matter. By the time they got around to investigating the anomaly, the worm would already be released and buried beneath lines of code.

She bent down and inserted the memory stick. The light on the port glowed and Drake made a satisfied grunt.

"Just another few seconds," he said.

Rainey heard mad clicking from his keyboard. Then she saw movement in her peripheral vision. She stood and walked away from her targeted rack.

A head topped with messy curls peeked around the corner. "I thought I saw somebody."

She continued moving toward him and gave a casual wave.

"How long you been at it?" he asked. His face didn't betray any suspicion, but that didn't mean anything. She was trained to keep her face under control, too.

"Just came on shift."

"Two days straight for me." He did look bleary-eyed. "I was finishing up a code before I left, but a whole rack just sent off an alarm."

Rainey's stomach knotted up. She didn't want to hurt this guy. "Oh?"

"Everybody else had already escaped, so the boss sent me down." He pointed toward the far wall.

"Too bad," Rainey commiserated.

"Gotta run. Blasted Russians."

"Tell me about it."

He gave her a wave and rushed off.

Rainey walked back toward her rack of servers.

"All done." Drake's voice startled her. "Take the thumb drive."

Right, like she was going to leave it. Rainey bent down and pulled the memory stick out of the port, stuffed it into her bra again, and headed out, remembering to retrieve her cell phone on the way.

# 3

"You've got to be kidding." Rainey stared at the tinted contact lens on the tip of the Gadget Master's finger.

"Yeah, isn't it exciting? The camera and mic are embedded in the lenses," he said. "We can see and—"

"No, that's not what I mean. It's blue."

"That's what . . ." His other hand came up in the air and he tried to look at everyone in the room at once. Other agents assigned to this op were getting fitted and not paying any attention. "The order was . . . did we get it wrong?" He was only interested in his spiffy new technology and hadn't worked the rest of it out yet. Then he looked back at Rainey and his eyes went wide. "Oh."

She snorted.

A man in a blue pin-striped suit stepped forward. "I'm Eric Tinburn. Liaison from the FBI."

Rainey nodded her head without offering her name. Old habit. This was the problem working with several agencies. Too many people and confusion reigned. She needed her anonymity.

"That's the idea," Eric explained. "We want you going into this white supremacy group with the most protection we can offer."

A potpourri of conflicting emotions competed for Rainey's attention. By now, her training was so deep she was certain nothing showed on her face. "You do realize some of their members are black and Latinx. Even Asian."

"Very few." Tinburn shrugged off her objection. "We're just following orders."

The Gadget Master started to speak, but Rainey held her palm up to stop him.

Their target was the Sons of Liberty. A dangerous group, formed about fifteen years ago in Virginia from a group of disgruntled right-wingers after President O'Connor's election. They'd grown over the years, connecting with militias in other states, creating a network that now worked closely together. At least, that was the theory. Many had taken their name from a group of loosely organized bands that had worked against taxation leading up to the Revolutionary War.

"Loosely organized" described this current movement as well and that was the problem. The usual social media and cell phone tracking had not uncovered the full picture. The Russian hack into sensitive databases complicated the situation further. Rainey would go in with a group of agents, their mission to plant some backdoors into their tech and to do a bit of old-fashioned spy work. She was supposed to catch the eye of their leader. Get close enough to grab his phone and clone it. Then Drake would have access. Maybe camouflage was a good idea.

On the other hand, Rainey had her pride. She resented the suggestion she couldn't handle herself in any situation she found herself in. But she was still thinking like an assassin. And that wasn't the assignment.

"I'll wear it."

"Best tech. Best camouflage." The Gadget Master returned the contacts to their little plastic case.

"I understand, Q."

"So, now I'm that guy who started all this?" he asked, hands on his hips.

Rainey sputtered a laugh. "No, no. I meant the guy in *I Spy.*"

"I swear, you and Control. Always with the spy shows." He studied her with a frown. "But you got that one mixed up with James Bond. Q was in the 007 movies."

Rainey threw up her hands. "There are too many to keep up with."

"Anyway, you're not old enough for *I Spy*."

"I had to figure out what Control kept talking about. I watched them on Nick at Night."

"I see. Well, my name is Sam. As in Samson. You know his story, right?"

Rainey gave him a wicked look. "Where are the scissors?"

"Speaking of hair." He held up a wig. A blond wig.

"No way," Rainey said.

"Oh, yeah."

"So what does the wig do?"

Sam's forehead crinkled in confusion.

"If I go in for a kiss and pull on my earlobe, does it spray out sodium pentothal?"

"Good one," Sam said. He put the wig back into a small suitcase, then waved for her to follow him. "I think you'll be more comfortable with the rest of your ensemble. Let's go pick out your weapons."

"Now you're talking."

---

AROUND SIX THAT EVENING, Rainey met the team back at the black site. Five operatives in all. If she didn't know they were dressed for this Sons of Liberty meeting, she wouldn't have gone in the room. Partly, it was what she would expect from neo-Nazis—skin heads, motorcycle club jackets, big belts with pockets for knives. But along with her new identity, the packet she'd received from headquarters contained a plethora of information on right-wing militia groups, from their philosophy all the way down to the meaning of their fashion choices.

One guy sported a leather jacket with the Black Sun on the back, a common neo-Nazi symbol adapted from a floor mosaic in Heinrich

Himmler's SS Generals' Hall of the Wewelsburg in Büren. The image would appear innocuous to most people. An interesting emblem—maybe from the Vikings or India. Another wore a beige polo shirt with a circular logo, preppy except for 88 inside the circle, neo-Nazi code for "Heil Hitler."

She had donned her own costume, complete with blue contact lenses and dusky blonde wig. Her fawn skin made her look like she'd spent a week at the beach. They'd given her a fluffy dress and, the worst part yet, wedge shoes that put her a bit off balance. Damn things were clunky, but easy to kick off if she had to fight or run. She felt like she should add a cowboy hat and chew on a piece of straw to complete the look.

Eric Tinburn walked to the front of the large room and stood in front of the group with his legs spread and arms behind his back at parade rest, revealing his military background. Rainey wondered if Tinburn's stance was intentional or simply an unconscious habit. Another man stood just behind him, slighter, more dapper, and three times shiftier. He wore his hair in a stylish coif, in contrast to the FBI man's buzz cut. Definitely CIA.

Tinburn's voice cut through the low buzz of conversation. "I assume you all have committed your packets to memory and know more than you ever wanted to about these terrorist militia groups."

One man lowered his head to study his shoes, but the rest remained stone faced.

Rainey glanced around from her place against the wall in the back. She wondered if some of them had already known a lot about these groups. Maybe were secretly members. But the CIA would have found that out. At least she hoped so. Control would have for sure.

"We know at least three militia groups are meeting tonight. Intelligence suggests they're fund raising. And three on one night? Whatever they're planning will go down soon."

Rainey saw a few nods. What Tinburn said made sense.

"Tonight is meet and greet. Group One."

Rainey listened up. This was her assignment.

"Our main target is Jack Patrick, head of the Sons of Liberty Mili-

tia." Tinburn clicked a remote and Patrick's face appeared on a screen
behind him. He wore no shirt and a handkerchief around his head,
masking the color of his hair or absence thereof. His beard was a
dirty blonde mixed with gray. Straight nose, blue eyes. He scowled at
the camera. Still heavily muscled with a mandala tattoo on his left
shoulder. Rainey had a feeling he was posing for possible recruits. Or
a dating app.

"Your job is to make a solid connection to someone in the group.
Suzie—" He looked around.

On hearing her code name, Rainey gave a little salute, then
pushed the blond hair that swayed with the movement out of the way.
She'd have to get used to this wig.

"You'll get access to Jack Patrick's phone."

She nodded.

"Theo, you'll be going to Patrick's home to find his computer."

"Roger that," a man with big shoulders and trim hips answered in
a clipped voice.

"Juan, you're eyes for Theo."

"Yes, sir." Juan looked like an accountant wearing the wrong
outfit, but Theo fit right in with his crew cut and scar running across
his left cheek.

Rainey wondered what their real names were.

"Andy and Rick, you're with Suzie. Make some friends. Keep an
eye out for Suzie getting in too deep."

Rainey stopped herself from rolling her eyes.

"Our pleasure." Andy eyed her from head to toe.

A shiver of revulsion washed over Rainey. *Great, just great,* she
thought.

"Questions?"

The team looked around at each other. Nobody spoke up.

"Let's roll," Theo said.

"Group Two," Tinburn called out as Rainey's unit marched out to the
parking lot behind the building where their two vehicles were parked.
Theo's men got the standard black SUV. Rainey held back while Andy

and Rick vied for who was going to drive the Ford F-150 truck. Andy won out. Big surprise there. Rick took shotgun, his long legs stretched out in frayed jeans. Andy adjusted his black leather jacket that matched his dark hair and beard, probably thinking he would turn some female eyes tonight. Rainey jumped in the back of the full-sized cab.

Andy tore off, taking the turns fast enough to make the tires squeal a few times, marking himself as an amateur. Rick caught her eye in the mirror on the passenger vizor and gave a slight shake of his head. Apparently, he agreed with her assessment. Andy turned onto the freeway, heading south, and settled back.

"So, Suzie, what's your story?" Andy asked.

"Just got called for this mission," she said. "And you? You look like somebody who's seen some action." She bet he couldn't resist the chance to brag.

Rick snorted and glanced in the mirror. Rainey kept her face blank, but the twinkle in her eye must have given her away. He gave her a quick wink.

"We're both from Homeland. Worked some international terrorist cases together."

"Do tell," Rainey said. Best to keep him talking so he wouldn't ask about her.

"It's all need-to-know, unfortunately. Let's just say we had a hand in tracking Qassim al-Seif." He waited for her responses, then prompted her. "You know, the Al-Qaeda leader in Yemen."

"Wow." Rainey let her eyes go wide.

Rick waited a beat, then changed the subject. "Everybody clear on this mission?"

"Piece of cake. Just get the good ole boys talking. Gather intel," Andy said.

"I'm thinking I'll lift his phone after the speech," Rainey said. "People are going to mob him, try to shake his hand, get noticed."

"Good plan," Rick said.

"So, if you two could add to the chaos, that would help."

"Sure thing," Rick said.

"Unless I'm in deep with a potential CI." Andy gave her a cautioning look.

"The phone is a priority," Rick said. Clearly, he was the senior of the team.

They drove in silence until Andy took the next exit off the highway.

"Turn right and go through the next two lights," Rick directed. They didn't want to risk switching on the GPS. No need to be easy to find.

Rainey leaned forward. "I shouldn't be seen arriving with you. Let me out a few blocks away."

They passed the two lights, then Andy turned onto a side street near their destination.

"There. Under those maple trees," Rainey said.

"Maples?" Andy asked.

"See the clump of trees just ahead? Park under them."

Andy pulled over.

"Turn off the interior lights."

Rick reached up and clicked off the dome and map lights. Rainey grabbed her purse and slid out of the car. She tapped the roof of the truck and stepped into the shadow of the trees.

As she walked, Rainey pulled her legend over her, becoming Suzie. She was from Texas. Dropped out of college because the professors had been too liberal. Had worked a series of jobs from waitress to retail. Living off her daddy's dime. She was just back from Puerto Vallarta.

Rainey joined the line of people entering the meeting hall, listening to the banter around her. The new conservative news outlets that had sprung up to the right of the more familiar propaganda station pushed vaccine fears. The general consensus among the left was that this was an attempt to sabotage President Murray's economic agenda. If the economy didn't recover soon enough after the global pandemic, the Senate and House might swing back to Republican control. Fewer vaccinated people meant more variants of the virus and more sick people.

"That damned Chinese lab engineered the vaccine, you know. I wouldn't let them inject that poison into me. No siree."

"That stuff's got foreign DNA in it. It'll make you impotent."

Rainey bit her lip to keep from laughing.

"Guys, he's back!" shouted someone from behind her. "There's a new drop."

People scrambled to get a look at his phone, pulling against his arm and trying to peek over his shoulder.

>R !!TcQl7okW709/27/21 (Wed) 22:06:29 ID: 8e583d (5) No. 9458091>

>>2.00001

Upgrade.

Reload.

You thought this was over?

17 moves to 18.

R

"Whoopee!" the man with the phone shouted. "I knew it. 1776 was just the beginning."

A man in an old red hat from President Earl's first campaign pointed at the man's phone. "R? Who's that?"

"Don't you see?"

The man shook his head no.

"17. That's his old number in the alphabet. He's moved one up to R."

"You think?"

"Of course. An upgrade. 2.0. Get it?"

The man shrugged. Rainey wondered who was really behind the post, but these people were ready to believe their hero was back.

The line of people reached the door and Rainey dodged around the knot of conspiracists. She marched into the medium-sized auditorium and headed for the front, weaving between round-bellied men and others with rock-hard abs. Maybe this was how to pick out the active military in the group, she thought. She'd bet on close to seventy-five percent accuracy based on fitness level alone, at least those still fighting and not sitting behind a desk.

Closer to the front, two men stood on either side of the aisle guarding the first few rows. Rainey added a little sway to her hips, then came to a stop in front of the younger one.

"Front seats are reserved, miss."

"Oh, but I was so hoping to get up close to Mr. Patrick." Rainey touched her neck, enticing his eyes down. She took a deep breath, letting her breasts rise. The man's eyes dropped from her throat to her chest.

"Yes, ma'am, but we do need to save these seats for our major donors."

"Hmm—" Rainey put a little husk in her voice and lowered her eyes to the bulge in the man's jeans. "I do appreciate a large donor."

The man flushed red and sputtered out a laugh. "Yes, ma'am. Well . . ."

"My father donates quite a bit."

"And his name is?"

"Well, I can't really say. You know, he has an important job in the uh—" She tilted her head toward a man wearing a tattered army jacket.

"All right, then. What's your name?"

"I'll find you later . . ." She waited for him to supply his name.

"Peter."

She raised an eyebrow. "That name suits you."

His smile widened and he stepped aside. "See you later, then."

"Count on it." Rainey sashayed down the aisle and took the first seat in the third row. From here she could catch Patrick's eye, but create mystery with a little distance.

The crowd grew boisterous as the seats filled. She listened to the snippets of conversation in case she'd catch anything of interest, but most of the people here were not high enough in the organization to know much and the ones in the front rows too savvy to talk in public. The new drop seemed to dominate the conversation, proving that the election had been a fraud and their anonymous hero was back to lead the charge.

A little beep in her ear caught her attention, then Drake's voice whispered, "Testing. Testing. Are you receiving?"

"Hm huh," she murmured.

"Great. I'll be listening in. I'm sure it will be inspiring and filled with facts."

Rainey tightened her jaw. Drake loved doing this—chatting away when he knew she couldn't respond.

"To review."

She didn't need a review.

"We'll try remotely first. Pull up the app I designed on your own device now. When he comes out, I'll try to gain access. How close are you? Let me see." His voice drifted off. "Second row?"

"Will they start in three minutes, do you think?" Rainey asked the man sitting next to her.

He frowned at her specific number. "Soon enough."

"I can't wait," she said, hoping she didn't sound too much like a teenager.

The man nodded, then looked back at the stage. The spotlight came on. "I guess we don't have to wait any longer."

"Third row, then. That should be close enough," Drake said.

An older man wearing a Hawaiian shirt in eye-watering orange and purple walked from backstage and took the microphone out of its stand. One of the militia groups wore these kinds of shirts. She couldn't recall the name. There were a surprising number of organizations.

"Patriots. Nationalists. Defenders of the constitution," he shouted.

A tremendous cheer came up from the crowd, louder than what Rainey thought this crowd could generate.

"You all know why you're here. We're living in a pivotal moment. They're giving our country away. You work hard to support your families, but these libtards are just handing out money to people who are too lazy to work. Too stupid to make their own way in the world.

They don't believe in our country. They've opened the borders to criminals, rapists, murders."

A huge boo filled the room.

"Bringing in diseases."

More shouts.

"And the only one who had the nerve to say it out loud? They killed him."

The crowd growled its anger, sounding like an enraged, hungry beast.

"Murdered him in cold blood."

The crowd surged to its feet and started shouting, "Find the killer. Find the killer."

*I'm right here,* she thought.

Except she hadn't killed him. He'd done her a favor and keeled over right there in front of her and the thirteen-year-old he had tied to the bed.

The warm-up speaker waved his fist in the air. Then held his palms up and pushed them toward the floor. The crowd took a while to quiet down. "You know what we need to do. We can either take our country back now or lose it forever."

"They will not replace us." A few people started the chant in the back and the group soon took it up.

The man on stage let it taper off.

"And here to tell us how to take our country back is our leader, Jack Patrick."

The cheer was deafening. Rainey stood and shouted along with the crowd, waving her fist in the air.

Her target walked on stage.

# 4

Grant Mendez found himself sitting in the middle of a shouting, jostling crowd, hunched over so he'd be as invisible as possible. The bald guy at the front was raving on. "We are smarter. Our ancestors spread through the globe and subdued the savages. Brought them civilization."

A few cheers went up.

"But did they appreciate it?"

"No," several voices shouted.

"We are the master race and we've been displaced from our natural leadership of the world."

Frank Foley, leader of the Patriot League, stopped and stared at everyone, the pregnant pause building tension. The guy knew how to work a crowd. Grant would give him that.

Then he almost whispered and everyone leaned in to hear. "The powers that be think our demonstration after the election was the main event."

Jeers rose from the crowd.

He shouted, "But we have a surprise in store for them."

Half the audience surged to their feet with a roar, waving their fists in the air. Grant waved his so he'd blend in.

A chant rose up. "You will not replace us." The crowd repeated it for a while until the guy at the front made a gesture to quiet them. Apparently, he had more to say.

Grant had come to the meeting of the Patriot League after his group commander, Brad Rogers, had started to make thinly veiled threats. "My team needs to get on board," he kept repeating.

"I ain't puttin' up with this crap," Derrick said when he told Grant he was leaving Red Sky, the private military contractor that had recruited them from Army Special Forces. Derrick had left two months ago. The fact that he was black seemed to have escaped Brad's notice, just like he didn't realize that Grant's family was among the original settlers in Colorado when it had still been Mexico. The men surrounding Grant now certainly didn't think he belonged in the master race. He was a touch on the brown side. Grant missed Derrick. He'd been his best friend.

The group sat back in their seats. Grant squinched down in his seat, trying to go unnoticed in the crowd of heavily muscled and mostly armed white men. He'd spotted some darker faces in the crowd. A few Latinos with the look of men who worshipped the machismo credo. Even two African Americans shouted as enthusiastically as the skinheads. He didn't understand it.

Grant thought about Derrick's decision. It had been tough. Red Sky's pay was hard to beat. The training was top notch, and they had a good amount of down time between assignments. Grant had just bought a nice place in Woodfield close to Fort Bragg and was dating Alicia pretty steady. Derrick had still been renting.

The man next to Grant rammed the butt of his AR-15 into Grant's leg. Again. Hard enough to leave a bruise this time. The guy had brought the rifle to the meeting for some inexplicable reason and didn't seem to know how to handle it. Grant tried to shift away without bringing attention to himself, but the man remained oblivious. He responded to the speaker, raising his fist and shouting, and hit Grant's leg once more.

He hoped the rifle wasn't loaded. If this guy was any indication, the group didn't stand a chance against the troops they'd go up against. But Grant knew there were others. A lot of private military contractors had joined the uprising, plus some retired military and law enforcement people. Others who were still actively serving. At least they still had jobs today. Grant wondered what was taking the FBI so long to find them all.

His phone vibrated. He pulled it out of his pocket and thumbed it on. A message from Brad popped up.

*Meet me in back.*

Grant was relieved when the speaker shouted, "Find Charles Earl," and the crowd took up the chant, many surging to their feet. One theory held President Earl had been kidnapped and was still alive. Grant took the opportunity to slip out of his row without calling too much attention to himself.

In the back, Brad stood talking to an older man who wore a green plaid flannel shirt, jeans, and hunting boots. His beard was neatly trimmed, gray with streaks of dark brown just like his hair. Something about him was familiar, but Grant couldn't put his finger on it.

Brad gestured toward Grant. "Here's one of my squad. Grant, you remember General—"

The man coughed in warning and Brad changed course, "This is . . ."

"Jet Prince," the man said.

"Right." Brad shook his finger in the air.

Brad turned to Grant. "You might remember him from our time in Kandahar."

Grant recognized the general now, but couldn't recall his real name. His urge to salute almost won out, but he grabbed the side of his pants and kept his arm down by his side. He gave a clipped nod. "Sir."

Prince returned the nod and studied him. The eye contact lasted a little too long for Grant's comfort. He tried to hold still under the scrutiny. Finally, the man broke his silence. "You comfortable with all this, Lieutenant Mendez?"

Grant wondered if he'd imagined the slight emphasis on his last name. "Yes, sir." His response was automatic. Trained into him. Except he didn't know exactly what he was supposed to be comfortable with. Maybe this meeting?

Brad chuckled, which pissed Grant off for some reason.

"My family settled this country. They came here in the 1720s." Pride swelled in Grant's voice.

"Is that right?" the general said, raising an eyebrow in surprise.

"Yes, sir. They came from northern Spain, which is still in Europe as far as I know."

The general gave a short bark of a laugh and slapped him on the shoulder. "Well, all right then. You're on board?"

"I haven't filled him in on the details, sir. I was waiting for your go ahead," Brad said.

The general nodded. "Good man. Lt. Mendez here passed the security check. I just like to look a man in the eye before briefing him on the plan to save this great nation—" he looked back at Mendez "—which your family helped found."

The knot in Grant's stomach loosened a bit. "Thank you, sir."

"Get him up to speed, then."

Brad's hand was halfway to his forehead before he caught himself. He stuffed it under his other arm, looking awkward. But nobody was watching them. They were all shouting about how the media had lied about President Earl's demise.

---

RAINEY ACTIVATED the app on her phone as soon as Jack Patrick walked on stage. She managed to catch his eye early into his rant and reeled him in with her rapt expression and loosely buttoned blouse. She bit her lips to make them red and swollen, mussed her wig a bit, and let her dress to rise up her thighs. It all seemed to add fuel to his fire.

"You all know the election was stolen," he shouted. "Our candidate didn't win because they let immigrants and dead people vote. They threw away ballots marked for Hoffman."

Jeers and boos rose from the crowd.

"They stopped the recount with their activist judges. Now, when we're trying to protect our voting rights, they accuse us of trying to take theirs away."

The men around Rainey jumped to their feet and the crowd chanted, "Stop the thieves. Stop the thieves."

Rainey cheered and waved her fist.

Patrick marched back and forth on the stage, a huge smile on his face. He glanced over at her and nodded approval. The chant continued, so he raised his hands for quiet. The group complied, eager to hear more.

"We're not done," he said in a quieter voice. "We won't let them take our country. The people who founded this great nation were Christians."

The crowd stayed on their feet, repeating his words. "Christians."

"They were Europeans." He looked out at everyone.

"Europeans," they shouted back.

"You know what that means." His voice grew louder with each phrase.

"All lives matter. All lives matter."

Patrick waited them out. When they quieted, he said, "We need to keep our heritage."

He paused and the crowd waited for his next words. "But we need your support."

A few people cheered. Rainey waved her fist.

"This time we're not advertising our plans. But you're smart people. You can put two and two together."

More cheers rose.

He looked at the ground and shook his head as if ashamed. Then he stared out at the audience again. "We've got big plans, but we're strapped for funds. We need your donations to pull it off."

There was a moment of silence, then a man shouted. "Hell yes, brother. I support you."

Rainey wondered if he was a plant from the Sons of Liberty.

"I've got your back," someone else shouted. Rainey turned to see a man in red flannel surge to his feet, his face matching his shirt.

More followed him.

Patrick let his eyes tear up. He put his hands together and raised them up. "Thank you, Lord. Thank you for these patriots. I promise you we will not disappoint them."

Rainey stopped herself from rolling her eyes.

The crowd surged to their feet, shouting their approval. Soon a chant rose. "They will not replace us." Over and over.

Patrick let them shout. The chant went on and when it started to fade, he waved his fist and the crowd started up again. The auditorium rang with voices for at least five minutes.

When everyone started to settle down, he said, "Dig deep, brothers and sisters. Help us make sure we keep our nation pure. The lovely ladies in the back have donation baskets for you. Believe me, we won't forget you."

After another burst of applause, people started getting up to leave. Many reached into their back pockets for their wallets. Women opened their purses. Rainey joined the flow of people making their way out, blending in.

Patrick walked down the left aisle. She made sure her phone was still activated and shadowed him, staying hidden in the crowd. A few people stopped him to talk, some to pound him on the shoulder.

She palmed the new SIM card she was supposed to put in his phone as a backup plan if the electronic signal didn't work.

Drake's voice sounded in her ear. "Try to get closer."

When the crowd thinned, Rainey slipped down a line of chairs and came out behind Patrick. The man talking to the leader took up the whole aisle, so she moved close.

"No good. Can you get your hands on his phone?"

Rainey examined Patrick's backside, feigning interest in what was beneath his jeans. Both back pockets of his pants bulged. One lump was square, the size of a wallet. The other longer and thinner. Patrick was busy talking to the cluster of people in front of him. His security was scanning them.

She reached for his phone.

"Can I help you, Miss?" Rainey looked up into the face of one of Patrick's bodyguards.

*Oh, shit.*

Just in time, Patrick turned around and saw her. "You."

Another spike of alarm ran through Rainey.

He pointed his finger at her. "I saw you towards the front, right?" His voice was husky, maybe strained from all that shouting, but Rainey doubted it. He was definitely interested.

"You noticed me?" Rainey added an aw-shucks tone to her voice.

"I certainly did."

"Why thank you, sir." She looked up through her lashes. He was tall. "I certainly noticed you."

"Nice tan. Where've you been?"

"I was on the beach in Puerto Vallarta for a week. I just love the sun." N3Mo had laid down a cover trail for her. It should all check out.

"It looks good on you. What's your name?"

"Suzie, sir."

Patrick hooked his thumbs into the belt loops on his pants and smiled down at her. A man beside him cleared his throat and others pressed to get closer.

"I wanted to give you my number if that's not too forward," she said with a sugar-sweet Southern accent, "but you're so popular. Everybody wants to speak with you."

"I like a woman who knows what she wants." Patrick pulled his phone from his back pocket. "What's your number?"

Rainey looked around at the crowd, then whispered, "I don't want to give it to everybody."

Patrick laughed. "Right."

"I could call you," she suggested.

"Same problem," Patrick said in a low voice. "I'll tell you what—"

He pressed his thumb to the home button on his cellular and started to hand it to her.

His bodyguard took an audible breath and leaned forward, but Patrick waved him off.

"There he is. Jack Patrick," somebody shouted at the edge of the crowd. Rainey looked up to see the man in the red flannel shirt pushing people out of his way to get to his hero. He pushed an older woman into Patrick, knocking him off balance. Patrick fell against his bodyguard and dropped his phone.

The bodyguard stepped back to catch Patrick, knocking against Rainey. She went down and her phone and the SIM card skittered across the floor under the row of chairs.

Rainey crawled under the seats, searching for her phone. She found discarded cups and food wrappers. People were eating in here? Her hand came down in something sticky. Disgusted, she wiped it on a crumpled flyer.

"I can't find the phone," she said in a low voice, hoping Drake could hear her.

"Calling now," Drake said.

A light came on under a chair in the row behind her, accompanied by a small ring tone. She scooped up the phone and found the SIM card lying next to it.

*Thank God.*

"Got it," she told Drake.

She stood up and brushed herself off. Looking around for Patrick, she saw him surrounded by his bodyguards. Mr. Red Flannel was pushed up against a wall. The crowd buzzed angrily around him.

"You have no manners, sir." The woman who'd fallen into Patrick had her finger in the offender's face. "You almost made me hurt Mr. Patrick."

Rainey's foot pushed against a hard object and she looked down. There lay Patrick's phone. She couldn't believe her luck. She grabbed it, pulled out his SIM card, and quickly replaced it with the new one.

Breathing a sigh of relief, Rainey held the phone up in the air. "Well, I found my iPhone. Did someone lose a Samsung?"

"I do believe that's mine," Patrick said.

She walked over and held it out to him.

"Did you give me your number?"

Rainey laughed, imitating an airhead. "I completely forgot."

"If you'd do me the honor," Patrick said.

"Sir," his bodyguard started to object.

"It's all right."

Rainey entered her burner number into his Samsung. "Your speech was just brilliant, Mr. Patrick."

"Call me Jack."

"Are you sure?" She handed the phone back to him, letting her index finger draw a light line down his palm as she withdrew her hand.

He looked at the display, then typed in her name as he said it. "Suzie. . ." He raised an eyebrow expectantly.

"Jones, sir." She'd used Jones too often lately. Better switch it up next time.

He pointed a finger at her. "Jack, remember?"

She flushed. "Jack."

"You'll be hearing from me, Suzie Jones."

She gave him her best perky smile. "Looking forward to it."

Rainey melted back into the crowd, the adrenaline leaving her shaky. She knew from experience it would pass.

*We're in,* Drake said a few seconds later.

Rainey retraced her steps to the spot where the team had dropped her. The pickup arrived a few minutes later.

"How'd it go?" Rick asked as soon as she slid the back door closed.

"Mission accomplished."

"I'll say. You really hooked in old Patrick." Andy's suggestive tone made her feel oily. She hoped this was the last they'd work together.

"That was the job. How about you? Make any new friends?"

"One good ole boy may be in on the plan. I got his particulars," Andy bragged.

"Particulars?" Drake said in her ear.

She bit her lip to keep from laughing.

"Theo copied his hard drive," her hacker informed her.

"Good," she said.

"I thought so." Andy lifted his head, his face smug. She wondered how many missions he'd actually been on.

After the debrief, Rainey made it out without having to talk to anyone again. She'd shower off Patrick's eyes, Andy's insinuations, all that racial hatred, then get some takeout. Something ethnic. She felt rebellious. Maybe she'd watch more episodes of *I Spy* while she waited for Patrick's next move.

## 5

Rainey's burner rang and displayed the name of the only person outside her team who had this number: Jack Patrick.

*That was fast,* she thought. They'd only met the night before. She must have made an impression. Or something sinister was going on.

Rainey pushed that thought away and called up her best Southern accent. "Hello, this is Suzie."

"Suzie," Patrick's commanding voice sounded loud in her ear. "I'm glad I caught you. This is Jack."

Suzie would be coy. "Jack?"

"Jack Patrick. We met last night."

"Oh, Mr. Patrick. What an honor," she gushed.

He chuckled, sounding pleased with himself. "Well, thank you. Say, I know it's short notice, but I wondered if you're available for dinner tonight."

"My goodness. I'd love to, but I'll have to check."

"I've got some free time before I'm booked up for a couple of weeks and wanted to get to know you a little bit."

Rainey put him on speaker so he'd think she was examining her calendar. "I'm looking now." After a minute, she said, "You know, I can move a few things around. Tonight will work."

"Great! How about we meet at that farm to table place in Foggy Bottom? I'm texting you a link to their website."

The link popped up almost immediately. She clicked it. "Good choice."

His voice turned sultry. "Or I could have my chef whip us up something."

"Well, being it's a first date and all, I'll meet you at the restaurant around eight."

"I'm looking forward to it."

Control put Rick on surveillance for the date. Not that she needed protection. He would check for known associates, keep eyes and ears on the room. To Rainey's relief, Andy had another assignment, so Juan was tasked to watch the area surrounding the restaurant. The three of them studied schematics from blueprints online, then checked out the place around four. Rainey didn't need any camouflage since Suzie was a disguise, but Rick and Juan donned blue suits and talked about the senators they allegedly worked for.

Glass doors in front opened to an enormous space, creating excellent visibility to most areas of the restaurant. A bar ran down one side with a colorful display of bottles on the mirrored, back lit wall behind. Since it was a late summer, more glass doors opened to patio seating. Lots of exits. The place backed to a courtyard. A low stone wall separated tables from the sidewalk. Rainey got a peek at the kitchen, which was equally large. A narrow hallway led to the restrooms.

"Piece of cake," Rick said.

"Maybe, but it's like Swiss cheese," Juan said. "People could approach from several sides and she could get swamped."

"Do we need another team member?"

Rainey shook her head. "I'll be fine."

AROUND SEVEN THAT EVENING, Rainey donned a dress with a twirly skirt and some fancy cowboy boots along with her blond wig. She pushed the makeup, adding more eye shadow and finishing off with bright lipstick, which she ordinarily never wore.

Patrick was already seated when she arrived, wearing clean jeans and a pressed blue work shirt. Keeping up his image, she imagined. He stood when the hostess ushered her to their table, located in the back to give a hint of privacy. He looked her up and down, then captured her eyes, their color changed by the blue lenses. "Beautiful."

She gave a little curtesy. "Why thank you, sir."

He held out her chair and she sat. "Find the place all right?"

"No problem." She hung her tan leather purse on her chair and leaned her arms against the table. "Good American food, I see."

His eyes lit up. "Nothing better."

They studied the menu. When their waiter came, Patrick took it upon himself to order appetizers—cornbread and dates wrapped in bacon. He ordered fried chicken for himself and was about to say 'and also for the lady' when she intervened.

"If you don't mind, I want to try that ravioli with the butternut squash. I just love that stuff."

Patrick dipped his head, then looked back up at the waiter. "Let's have that Napa Valley chardonnay."

The waiter hurried off to put in the order.

"So, we're drinking liberal wine?" Rainey joked.

Patrick's laugh rumbled in his chest. "We have some members from that area. They're not all deluded."

"That's good to hear."

The appetizers arrived and Rainey kept Patrick talking about himself and his activism, as he called it, so much so that he didn't notice her avoiding the bacon. Ever since her last visit to Tibet, she'd decided to go vegetarian. She wasn't a fanatic about it, but she didn't like to think another being suffered to feed her.

Ironic for an assassin.

"Enough about me," he said. "What about you? How'd you come to back us?"

"My daddy is a supporter. He raised us to understand our true place in the world." That last part was accurate enough. Her father had worked doubly hard to immigrate from India and make his way in the work world. When the tech bubble burst, he'd found a place with India Airlines because of his knowledge of the languages of the country and his computer skills. Hadn't blinked an eye at working for almost half his former salary.

The main course arrived and Patrick insisted she taste his chicken. So much for being a vegetarian tonight. She put her hand on his wrist to steady the leg he offered, noting a professional manicure and a Cartier watch worth several thousand. She took a dainty nibble, looking up at him through her lashes. His pulse surged.

"Hmm. Good?" he asked, his voice husky.

"Delicious," she mumbled around the bite of chicken.

Rainey turned the conversation to his early days in the group, what made him realize the "truth" about this country. He told her a story of his football days, how a black man—only he didn't use those words—stole his NFL offer. "You know they bred them for work, so it's no wonder they beat out the smarter whites. At least we're still the majority of the quarterbacks." He put the bone of his chicken leg down and studied his hands, gave her a quick glance, then wiped the grease off with his napkin. "The owners are white and rich."

Rainey nodded vigorously, swallowing down the rising bile. "How's the fundraising going?"

He paused before picking up his wine. "Really good. Better than I hoped."

"I sure hope y'all have more planned after the failure at the Capitol."

He swirled the last bit of wine, studying her. "That was a warning. I wouldn't call it a failure."

Before Rainey could respond, the waiter appeared. "Dessert?"

Patrick raised his eyebrows in question. Rainey hesitated, and he said in a low voice, "I've got chocolate mousse at the house that I ordered just for tonight."

She put her hand over her heart. "My favorite. How did you know?"

"I have my ways."

"Just bring the check," he told the waiter. Then looked back at her.

"Is that all we'll have for dessert?" she asked, her voice heavy with suggestion.

She hoped she could explore while she was there—ferret out what the group was planning. Spike his drink and loosen his tongue. The form email they sent to thank donors promised action.

Patrick slapped cash onto the table and stood. He looked at her, his eyes predatory for a second. A wave of revulsion rolled over Rainey. She'd seen that look in Afghanistan. But his ferocity was replaced with lust in a few seconds. She released her grip on the butter knife beside her plate. Whatever he had planned, she was certain she could take care of herself.

She insisted on following him in her car. He headed northwest, crossed the river near Georgetown, and drove along the other side. Just before they reached Windy Run Park, Patrick turned up a small road. At the end stood a white colonial on top of the hill. Patrick pulled his supped-up Ford truck into a converted barn. Rainey parked on the side of the driveway for an easy exit. She got out and walked toward the house. Motion detectors flipped on small lanterns that lined the walk, forming pools of light. She waited at the start of the path.

Patrick joined her, slipped his arm around her, and pulled her to him. "Suzie." He leaned down and pushed her hair away from her neck.

Rainey hoped she'd secured her wig properly.

He breathed in her scent, then kissed beneath her ear. Rainey leaned into him, noting the firm torso, muscled shoulders. His center of gravity was a little high. Good to know.

He ran his hand down her arm and claimed her hand, leading her to the house. He unlocked the door and gestured for her to go first.

She stepped into an entryway, her cowboy boots thudding on the slate floor.

Patrick flipped on the light switch. Her vision flooded with searing white light. She clamped her eyes shut.

*It's a trap.*

Footsteps rushed at her from inside the house. She ran forward to gain more space, then dropped into a crouch, switching her attention to sounds. Two to the right. Three to the front. Patrick in the doorway. More men rushed in behind him. At least three.

Damn. What had given her away?

Somebody from the left grabbed her arm. She stepped into him, letting him take her with him, then turned her hand and grasped the muscled forearm. She twisted his wrist as she fell. The sharp snap of a bone sounded, and the man dropped to his knees, howling in pain.

Two more rushed her, one on either side. Dark spots danced in front of her eyes as her sight started to recover. Shapes came more into focus. She surged up, bringing a palm heel to the nose of the one on the right. Blood ran down his chin. He stared at her, shocked, then dropped to the wood floor. Dead weight. The bone must have penetrated his brain.

Two down. How many to go?

Somebody from behind grabbed her wig and pulled it off. "Nigger bitch, thought you'd fool us, didn't you?" It was Patrick's voice.

The clips from the wig pulled her back, tearing out a few strands of hair. The sting brought tears to her eyes.

"Yeah, now you cry."

"Ain't going to do you no good, monkey." A different voice. He grabbed her purse and pulled it off her shoulder. Threw it far away into the living room, where she heard it land with a thud.

*Damn it. There goes my gun.*

She'd left her smaller pistol that she usually tucked into her waistband at home, anticipating close encounters of a different kind. Oh, well.

Rainey regained her balance and spun in a circle, assessing her opponents. That's when she saw him.

A man on her list.

Not Control's list, but the one she'd received on the other side during her near-death experience in Afghanistan.

The list had emblazoned itself on her mind. None of the men who'd killed her were on it. But she remembered those who were. Not necessarily as a list of names. Some, yes, but not all. She didn't always know who they were or why she was supposed to escort them to that tunnel of light—and they all went there, not to fiery torment —but when she saw one, she knew. Then their name would flash on her inner vision.

*Georg Fischer. Born in Argentina to second-generation German immigrants. His grandparents fled with other SS members when the allied army had crushed Hitler's forces. Bred on Nazi beliefs. Now high up in industrial espionage.*

All this information flooded Rainey's mind. She shook her head to clear it out, to focus on surviving her current situation.

The men circled her like a pack of hyenas, more wary now that she'd taken two of them down. She crouched, waiting for somebody to make a mistake. To move toward her or step off balance. For their attention to waver.

She didn't have to wait long. Two younger men on her right side started to taunt the others.

"What we waitin' for? She ain't nothing."

"Skinny as a rail."

She heard the fear in their voice. She feigned a move toward one and he jumped back. Embarrassed, he rushed her. His friend joined in. She grasped his incoming fist and dropped down. Used her momentum to jerk him toward his friend. Their heads slammed together. One fell to the floor, out cold. The other grabbed his head, eyes blinking.

Three down. One disoriented. For now.

Rainey moved to the stairs and kicked the spotlight over. Two more rushed her from the dining room. She dodged a punch to the head, but the second man got in a low blow to her kidney. She blew out her breath as the punch landed, then hit him with a flurry of fists, driving him back onto another man who was trying to get up the stairs. They piled onto the floor.

Rainey ran up the steps and opened the first door. A small guest bedroom. She closed the door, making enough noise to be heard, then went to the next door. Bathroom. She closed the door silently. The next door revealed a large master suite. Enough room to hide and fight in.

She tiptoed in, closing the door behind her, and looked for a hiding spot. Not under the California king sized bed. It was big enough, but awkward for maneuvering. The en suite had a soaking tub and large shower next to it, but with an all-glass enclosure.

"She's not in here," one man shouted from down the hall.

More voices came from that direction. A door opened. Some movement. "Clear."

So, there were some military men in the group.

Rainey came back out of the bathroom and rummaged through the drawers in the nightstand. A small pack of tissues. Eye drops. Several condoms. She went to the other side of the bed. A Rolex. Some loose change.

Ran her hand under the pillow. Bingo. A .357 Magnum revolver. She grabbed it, looked for ammunition. Found shells in the second drawer. Scooping them up, she headed for the walk-in closet. An obvious choice, but it was big.

The door to the bedroom opened. Quiet footsteps.

A row of belts hung from hooks on the back wall. She grabbed one. She moved behind a rack of suits. Nice fabric. Patrick had money and taste. She pushed the stray thoughts from her mind. She checked the revolver. Turning the cylinder to each chamber, she confirmed the weapon was loaded and pocketed the extra rounds. It was big and heavy. Awkward for her small hands.

The sliver of a mirror she could see from her hideout showed two men, one tall with dark hair, who put his finger to his lips. He pointed for the man on her list to check the bathroom. The dark-haired one moved around the bed, glanced in the closet, then dropped quickly to check under the bed. She pounced, slamming the back of his head with the gun.

He flattened out on the floor, unconscious.

The other man rushed from the bathroom, gun drawn. Georg Fischer. She aimed and shot. The weapon bucked, but held fast in her strong grip. Two to the chest.

"Shit. She's got a gun," someone shouted from the stairway.

Rainey focused back on Georg. He reached for his chest. Looked at her, maybe waiting for the head shot, but she didn't need it. She knew he had only seconds left. Then a sudden surprised look came over his face. She knew the tunnel of light had started to open to receive him. She didn't see it herself, but could feel his reaction. He reached out for it as he fell, dead when he hit the ground.

"Good journey home," she whispered.

She snapped a picture of his face for Drake to analyze. She apologized for the indignity. Then she moved through the room to the hallway. Did a fast check. Patrick was headed toward her, but he hadn't seen her yet. She ducked back into the bedroom.

The sound of wood splintering came from the front entryway, then shouts. "We're armed. The police are on their way."

Patrick looked back, then turned and ran down the hall in the opposite direction. He rounded a corner. She started to follow, but Juan appeared at the top of the steps. He swung around, gun pointed at her.

"It's me," she shouted, arms spread.

"Shit, almost clipped you."

"He went that way." She pointed to the hallway behind Juan.

"I'll follow him. Rick's in front."

"Where are the rest of them?"

"Scattered when I broke through the door. You check the back."

Rainey ran down the stairs and headed toward the rear of the house. The large kitchen opened to a family room. Rainey wondered if he had a family. The back door stood wide open. She moved to the side of it, looked around quickly, then moved out, gun pointed in front. The damn thing was heavy.

The motion detectors had lit up the spotlights on the back of the house, leaving sharp shadows beside bushes. The cover remained on the hot tub. Rainey crept out, keeping to the shadows. An outdoor grilling station and bar stood to the right. She ran to it in three steps and crouched behind the long counter. The area was still. Quiet.

She crawled to the end of the bar and took cover behind the hot tub. She jumped when the motor switched on and water swirled. She took a few deep, calming breaths and waited. Just a quiet hum. The tub was reheating, maintaining its temperature.

She moved into the shadow of bushes, senses open, alert for motion. The quiet remained. A Whippoorwill whistled from the woods beside the property. A car door slammed in back. The engine started.

A gunshot sounded from the same direction.

The engine roared and tires dug into gravel.

Another shot.

"Damn it." Rick's voice reached her across the stretch of yard.

Rainey made her way toward him, gun pointed down. "It's me," she said when he pivoted toward her.

"Missed the bastard."

"So I heard. What about the rest of them?"

"Scattered through the woods. Some made it to their cars and escaped while we were in the house."

"Let's grab his computer. Check his files. See what we can find."

The two walked back toward the house, setting off the spotlights again. Rainey held her hand up, fending off the glare. They found Juan in the office, already unhooking the computer. Rainey started on the files. She took everything that seemed to be related to the militias.

"Personal finance stuff?" she asked.

"Yeah, we might learn something."

She hauled a stack of files out to her car, then turned back for more. Rick walked out with another armful of paperwork and handed it to her. He slid Patrick's laptop onto the backseat. "Take these to the computer geeks. They can get started. Juan and I will finish up."

"Sounds good."

Rainey nosed her rental out of the driveway and started back to headquarters. She wondered if Patrick was watching somewhere in the trees. A few miles out, two Ford trucks passed her, bristling with rifles. Just as she was reaching for her phone, two black Escalades raced by. Government issued.

She punched in Rick's number. "Incoming. Two trucks. Six people. All armed. Two black SUVs are following them."

"Following or overtaking?"

"Don't know."

"We'll set up so we can figure it out."

"Roger that. See you back at the ranch."

## 6

"Georg Fischer, you say?" Drake asked. He finished loading Rainey's image and sent the computer on a hunt for more information.

"I think he's a plant. Maybe an industrial spy."

"What intel are you basing this on?"

Rainey couldn't exactly tell her colleague that she had a divine mission, a list handed to her from angelic beings. That he was one of her assigned targets. "When I saw him, I knew I'd seen his face in a file somewhere, but I can't quite remember."

"If that's true, we might be getting somewhere," Drake said.

Rainey took her seat in front of the bank of monitors covering a long wall of the large conference room and let her eyes roam over all the feeds. "Have we heard anything about those Escalades following the trucks into Patrick's property?"

Nobody answered her. Both hackers were intent on their laptops. N3Mo's spine curved like a question mark. Drake sat straighter, but was equally absorbed. She'd check it out herself.

Rainey touched the FBI feeds on her laptop. They expanded. She clicked on Militias, then the subfile Sons of Liberty. The last entry was two days ago. It listed donors and amounts with links to each donor's individual file.

Rainey poked around for a while, but found mostly ordinary citizens who'd bought the line that the Democrats had engineered President Earl's death and allowed illegal voting to elect Murray. Not to mention the child trafficking ring and sacrificing of infants. If they read any history, they'd see these types of accusations were standard fare.

She clicked her way out and entered the first four numbers of the license plate she'd caught a glimpse of into the search window. The plate number came up in a list of vehicles assigned to a general's office. General Steve Keegan. The name rang a bell. He'd been in charge in Kandahar. She'd just opened his office link when Drake came to life.

"Ah, here we go," he said.

Rainey shot out of her chair and leaned over Drake's shoulder. "What?"

He shook her off. "You know I hate people hanging over my shoulder.

"Actually, I didn't know. Sorry." She sat down beside him, giving him more space.

Drake started to read, "Georg Fischer. Born in Argentina. His grandparents fled with other SS members at the end of the war."

The hairs on Rainey's arms stood up. The words were so close to what had flashed across her mind when she'd set eyes on the man. It was uncanny.

"Bred on Nazi beliefs. Works for—" Drake rolled his chair around to face her. "Ready for this?"

"What?" Rainey demanded.

"Rosoil."

"Matvei Kiselev." She and Drake stared at each other.

Matvei Kiselev served as the CEO of Rosoil, Russia's largest oil and gas company. But everybody knew the Russian president Oleg Egorov ran the show. Rosoil came in tenth on the world's list of largest—and richest—oil companies, but these two Russians, along

with a handful of lesser oligarchs, were hard at work to move themselves up that list.

Oil money seemed to be behind all this mess, but what concerned
Rainey more was that Kiselev had sent an assassin after her during
her last assignment, the famed Vasil Dushku, better known as the
Albanian. Dushku had been on Rainey's list, and when he attacked
her at the presidential debates in Atlanta, she had come out the
victor. But Kiselev sent another man to eliminate her. Now it looked
like these same men were involved with the recent insurrection and
whatever they had planned next.

Drake swore he'd scrubbed any record of Rainey out of the
Russian SVR and Saudi computer banks. Also, the various oil
conglomerates' systems. It seemed like an impossible task, but she'd
seen Control's hacker pull off some pretty spectacular jobs. Most
likely this agent had nothing to do with her, but had been assigned to
work undercover with the militia.

Drake interrupted her train of thought. "This Georg is a Russian
agent."

Rainey nodded, then added almost as an afterthought. "Was."

The hacker made a wry face.

"Do you think he was the source of the leak about me?" Rainey
asked.

"Could be. Could be somebody on our side." He studied her for
another minute, his brown eyes clouded with worry. "What it does
mean is the Russians were involved in the insurrection attempt."

"And they're still working with the militias."

Drake nodded. "We've got some work to do."

---

ESEN AHMAD MOUTHED a Turkish curse under his breath when Georg
Fischer's face swam up on his computer monitor. Ostensibly the executive assistant for Kiselev's black ops, Esen had accepted the position
at the direction of Syed Burki, the Saudi Prince. The Prince and the
Russian president Egorov were in league together, but Burki didn't

trust the Russian. Esen's job was to observe and report secretly to the Saudis. The Turkish president also expected clandestine reports. He had too many masters.

Now he had to tell Kiselev about the death of an agent. At least he appeared to be dead. He'd have to confirm it.

Kiselev had looked pretty rough at their morning meeting. "We're close to going live and there's just too much to juggle," the man had yelled. "We've got lines into the FBI and CIA, but they keep failing. The three plants in Homeland are slow to report. At least we know about the two people in the militias. Except one of them might be a double agent." He slapped his shirt pocket, but didn't find his cigarettes.

Esen picked the pack up from the man's desk and held it out. Kiselev took one and waited for his assistant to light it for him. Esen suppressed a sigh as he flicked the lighter.

The executive assistant bore the brunt of it all, but he didn't say so. The boss's red eyes, unshaven cheeks, and rumpled suit spoke of the Russian's love of drink and young women. His breath still smelled of vodka. Esen wished the executive would go off on his yacht or to one of his houses in a big city and leave him to do his job.

Kiselev had been a professional at one time—sharp, competent, always on top of things. But too much power had eaten away at his character.

"We've got less than forty-eight hours before the operation starts. Keep me informed." Kiselev waved him away, ending their daily morning briefing.

"Yes, sir." Esen picked up his files and left, glad to get back to his desk.

After his meeting with Kiselev, Esen had spent the next two hours combing through intelligence summaries when this photo popped up.

Now, looking at the vacant eyes of Georg Fischer, Esen realized he had to report that one of their plants had been killed. It had taken a year of careful work for their agent to worm his way to the top of the Sons of Liberty. Another year before that to develop his accent and mannerisms, to train him in the intricacies of American politics. All down the drain right at the last minute.

First, he needed to confirm the kill, then find out as much as he could before he brought it to Kiselev. Esen downed his third Turkish coffee of the morning and set to work. He sent an encrypted text to one of their agents in the FBI, hoping he was awake. Even encrypted, he used their code.

*Fishing good this summer?*

While he waited for a reply, he navigated to the camera feeds from Georg's lapel pin. He watched the agent meet up with other men in what looked like a barn. The audio was spotty, but from what he gathered, they planned to terminate someone who'd infiltrated the organization.

After initial greetings and fist bumps, the group settled down to wait. Esen fast forwarded until he saw a blur of movement. He slowed down the replay and saw two men in front of Georg walking up the path to a house. The angle of the camera didn't give a good view, so it was difficult to tell where the group was. Esen grabbed the GPS coordinates off the feed and plugged them in to confirm what he already suspected. Jack Patrick's house.

Georg rushed in and the feed devolved into a melee of arms and legs, someone's back, the ceiling. Grunts and punches landing filled the soundtrack. Something getting knocked over. Georg headed up some stairs.

A ding alerted Esen to a text. He paused the replay and clicked on the message.

*Lost my best pole and reel. Need to replace it.*

Esen slumped in his chair. So it was true. One agent down. He hesitated to push play on Georg's camera, not wanting to see the man's last minutes, but maybe he could discover the identity of the infiltrator. He watched Georg walk down a hallway. His gun came into the picture. Georg entered a large bedroom. A larger than king-size bed and maple armoire dominated the room. The other man with Georg shouted muffled commands, but Esen couldn't make them out.

His agent turned right and entered a bathroom. Opened the cabinets beneath the double sinks. The rest was glass. Nobody hiding in there. He headed back out, and as he did, Esen caught a glimpse of Georg in the mirror. Compact build, brown hair neatly clipped, alert burnt umber eyes. In his prime. Esen felt a pang of sorrow.

A muffled cry sounded on the feed. Georg's head jerked up, and he ran back into the master bedroom. A slim woman looked up from a body slumped at the bottom of the bed. She raised a gun that was way too big for her. Must not be a professional. And shot twice. Georg's camera jerked up, framing his assassin, then pointed down.

The woman whispered something to him, then he fell. Her face swam into view as she riffled through his pockets. Rage filled Esen. He felt as if she were violating him as she searched the dead body of his agent. Esen rewound the recording and pushed up the volume. He listened carefully, but the words were muffled. He turned up the volume again.

"Good journey home." Her eyes filled with compassion and something else. Longing.

Esen jerked back. What the hell was going on here? Was this woman crazy? He captured a close-up of her from the feed. She was of medium height and well-muscled. Her skin was light beige and her hair hung in loose curls, damp with sweat. He enlarged a shot of her face and uploaded the image to a picture match program.

He sat watching the computer work. Not that he could see anything while it sorted through thousands of files in milliseconds. He could be checking other things, but finding her identity was the most important item on his agenda at the moment.

"Esen." Natalya, one of his deputies, stood by his shoulder. "What's the plan for the hearing?"

"Hearing?" He tried to bring himself back enough to remember what she was talking about.

"Do we have the schedule of witnesses yet?"

Ah, now he remembered. The U.S. Judicial Committee hearings investigating which officials had helped with the insurrection attempt. Esen got up and walked the woman back to her station.

"Babcock is supposed to confirm. Send him an email. See how quickly he answers."

Esen left Natalya at her desk and went into the men's room. He used the facilities and washed up, splashing his face to wake himself up. Maybe these long shifts were taking their toll. He couldn't remember the last time he'd slept a full night. Their next move was close. If it all worked as planned, maybe he could take a day after that. Fly down to the sea. Spend some time with his family.

Fat chance. As soon as the plan was executed, another set of problems would assert themselves. Hands braced on either side of the sink, he stared at himself in the mirror. He needed to send a message to the prince.

Esen pushed away from the sink, dried his hands, and walked back to Natalya's desk. "Got an answer?"

"Just came in."

"Can you print me a copy?"

Natalya looked surprised, but only hesitated a few seconds before hitting the print command. She handed the paper off to him as soon as the printer spit it out.

"I'll shred it."

"Of course, sir."

He had no intention of doing that. Some things were important enough to warrant keeping a paper copy.

Esen resisted the urge to get another coffee, knowing it would only make him jittery after he'd already had three this morning. He closed the door to his office and put the print-out on his old-fashioned ink blotter.

Damn it! The star witness was scheduled for tomorrow. They only had one day to mobilize and had lost an important asset.

His computer beeped. He glanced up at the screen, remembering his search for Georg's assassin.

*No results found.*

What? How could that be? The SVR servers had no record of this woman? He checked his search parameters. He'd gone wide.

Included the corporate computers plus the U.S. servers they still had backdoors to. He looked at the list. FBI, Homeland, Navy, Air Force.

He checked Interpol and again, the search came up with nothing.

Esen sat back, rubbing his finger across his temple. This didn't make any sense. Maybe she was British, but how did they get their fingers into this pie? He checked MI6—the areas he could access.

*No results found.*

Esen pulled up the woman's image again, staring at it for a few seconds. "Who are you?" he whispered.

Now was not the time for a rogue element. But there was no sense putting it off any longer. He pushed back from his desk and walked to Kiselev's office. Steeling himself, he knocked and, without waiting for an answer, opened the door a crack. "Got a minute?"

Kiselev's head shot up, a frown on his face. "What is it?"

"I'm afraid I have some bad news."

"Then come back tomorrow," Kiselev joked. He motioned for Esen to come in.

Esen entered and closed the door behind him.

Kiselev's eyebrows shot up. "That bad, huh?"

Esen got right to the point. "We lost Georg Fischer. He's been shot."

"Shot?"

"He's dead."

"What the fuck?" Kiselev slammed his meaty hand down on the desk. He stared out the window for a minute, then rubbed his forehead. He took a deep breath and said, "We're close. We can manage without him. The higher ups will be organizing within—" he glanced at his old-fashioned wristwatch "—twelve hours. Maybe more."

Relief washed over Esen. Kiselev seemed to have pulled himself together since this morning.

"Do we know who shot him?" his boss asked.

"Yes, sir." He woke up his phone—the mystery woman's picture swam up—and he handed it to Kiselev. "I can't find any intel—"

"*Suka, blyad.*" Fucking bitch. His boss surged to his feet.

"You know her, then."

"I know her." Kiselev's eyes were murderous. "You remember the Albanian?"

"Of course."

Vasil Dushku, known as the Albanian, had been the head of intelligence under Albania's president turned dictator and been charged with torture. Not just ordinary torture, either. Esen didn't like thinking about it. When President Berisha was deposed, Dushku had escaped the country before being apprehended. Finally arrested in London in 2012 where he'd been living under a false name, he escaped again and word had it he established a black ops group somewhere in the Mediterranean where he took contracts, doing extreme interrogation, assassinations, and gunrunning. The CIA and MI6 had tried for years to locate him, or so they said.

"And Boris Ivanov?" Kiselev asked.

Esen nodded. "One of our best operatives. Quite a loss."

Kiselev pointed his thick index finger at the picture on the phone. "She killed them both."

Esen jerked in surprise. "This little thing?" He indicated the woman with a tilt of his chin.

Kiselev held up his hand. "There's more. We have reason to believe she assassinated President Charles Jefferson Earl."

Esen shook his head, shocked to the core. "That's . . ."

"Impossible?"

Esen nodded.

"Did you find her file?"

"No, sir. There's nothing. I searched here, Interpol, the U.S., Britain. Searched the corporations. Came up empty."

"Fucking hackers," Kiselev spit out. He walked over to the wall and removed a painting by Levitan of a landscape, revealing a Protex wall safe. He put his thumb on a pad and waited for a beep, then moved his eye to a scanner next to the pad. A mechanism in the lock clicked. Kiselev opened the door and shifted through a stack of paper. He pulled out a manilla envelop.

"Always keep paper backup."

Esen smiled.

# 7

"I can monitor these feeds anywhere," Rainey said, already bored with watching the particular bank of screens she'd been assigned. She needed to move, do some forms outside. Breathe a little fresh air. Do her morning routine. Anything to get out of the war room Control had set up. But Control had grabbed her before she could slip out just before dawn.

After her adventure with Patrick, Control insisted she stay in the group's quarters. "You won't be in D.C. long enough to set up again. We'll need you at a moment's notice."

"I can be wherever you need me in less than no time," Rainey complained.

"There's a lot of activity in the militias," Control said, his voice patient and well-modulated. "We'll need to move in an instant."

"This kind of spy work is not my specialty."

Control steepled his fingers and studied her. After a minute, he simply said, "I appreciate your flexibility in this time of national crisis."

Somehow his cultured voice belied the phrase "national crisis." Didn't his class own the country? Actually, she wasn't sure of his class, but that well-heeled, transatlantic accent came through from time to time. He sounded very much like Grandmother Elizabeth Le Clair. And this house reminded her a bit of The Oaks, the Le Clair's ancestral home. At least on this side of the Atlantic. Rainey spent time there when she visited Arnold, who headed up the Le Clair family's security.

Control's lair was located close enough to Langley for emergency flights. She had a room at the top, complete with the odd angled ceilings of attic chambers. Control called it a farmhouse, but truth be told, it looked more like a colonial plantation, which made her just a bit squeamish. It was beautiful, complete with horses grazing on rolling hills, a swimming pool, and tennis courts. All for camouflage, of course. No tiny cabins that would indicate converted slave quarters. That helped. One barn had horses, but two more were full of cars, SUVs, Humvees, jeeps, and even a tank, plus a weapons armory that would make the marines green with envy.

Plus, the food was great. Control had a staff of chefs dripping with accolades as well as bacon grease. This morning she poked her head into the kitchen and the gleaming stainless steel of the walk-in refrigerator door, bank of ovens, and twelve-burner stove had practically blinded her. Her request for vegetarian fare had been greeted with, "but of course, mademoiselle," in a heavy French accent.

But she was stuck in the war room. Right now, Drake paced in front of the monitors, chewing on his lower lip. The displays showed Jack Patrick's computer and phone on the left, a position Rainey found ironic. Frank Foley's phone and the Patriot League computers came next, then the same for Nick Rangel of the Aryan Authority. At least this last group practiced honesty in advertising. She watched as the three organizations garnered donations from their fundraising events two nights ago. Some internal chatter among a secret faction about the death of Hank. Rainey figured that was Georg's undercover name.

One screen centered like a bull's eye on the wall was blank. It was designated for the FBI. Drake still waited to see if the hack she'd done on the agency's computers would pay off. Rainey thought it should have worked by now. Days felt like months in the middle of an op.

Oddly enough, the CIA computers were still accessible and their surveillance of current right-wing activities played out on two monitors above the one designated for the FBI. On the right, several A-2 senators and representatives were represented, as was Mr. Hoffman, the man who'd run against current President Murray.

The A-2 conspiracy theory had started with a rumor that the progressives were going to reverse the Second Amendment and collect all guns. It had rolled downhill from there, growing like a snowball, collecting wild claims as it went. The top billionaires in the world met every year to tell governments who their leaders would be. Various crime rings were attributed to the group, including child trafficking and drug running. It was taken for granted that liberals and Jews ran all the media, even some of the more conservative groups. The latest was that the flu vaccine would inject nanobots into your blood stream to track you.

*Like your phone doesn't already*, Rainey thought.

The new feed from R ran next to it. Drake and N3Mo figure this was the reincarnation of the one lettered idiot who'd worked people up into a frenzy over the last few years, then gone quiet. It sported just the one tweet. R had been silent since the fund-raising events, which made her mind speculate wildly about who he or she could really be.

The telephone rang in the outer office. Surprised, Rainey glanced at the time in the corner of one of the screens. Five past eight. It felt later and she wanted coffee. Usually, her run and Kajukenbo forms woke her up.

"Gaia Catering. We're here to serve you." After a brief silence, the secretary said, "Let me put you through to our event planner for weddings."

Apparently, that had been one of the rare legitimate inquiries. Control had connections with a few real businesses they referred to when they got such calls. They were told Gaia was just too busy to accommodate this particular order. One of these caterers was named Gaia Feasts, just to keep things more under wraps.

Rainey went back to watching the screens and Drake to pacing. He chewed on the knuckles of his right hand, his gaze roaming from display to display. A series of chimes sounded and Drake gave a grunt of satisfaction, pouncing on his laptop like it was a mouse that had crept out from its cover at long last. He clicked around and started to read, emitting little surprised hums as he did.

Finally he said, "You won't believe it."

"What?" Rainey asked.

"Dude, put it up on a screen." N3Mo's voice dripped derision as only a teenager's could.

"Maybe you're not cleared for—" Drake retorted, but before he could finish, the document flashed up to an empty screen on the far left.

And there it was. An undercover assignment for an agent to work as Frank Foley, current leader of the Patriot League. The document was dated two years ago.

"He's a plant." Rainey stated the obvious in a hushed voice.

"Indeed he is," Drake muttered. "I wonder . . . let's see what we can find." His fingers flew over the keyboard, a string of code unfurling on the monitor above, the teenager watching avidly.

"Wicked," N3Mo said.

Drake hit return. "Go get 'em."

In under a minute, a list of files appeared on the screen. N3Mo opened the first one.

"Would you stop?" Drake objected, but then started reading.

They worked their way through the downloads. Rainey went back to watching the other screens. Today was a big day in the Senate. The Judicial Committee had subpoenaed former Vice President Brian Hoffman to testify about his involvement in the rally that preceded the attack on the Capitol. Protests started when the committee had picked its investigators and grown in volume and threats as the group interrogated the police, various witnesses, then worked their way up the food chain to elected officials who'd cooperated with the group, sending out blueprints of the buildings and maps of the tunnels beneath, taking groups around to point out the offices of left-wing representatives and senators. Rainey still couldn't figure how these people who'd clearly committed sedition were still walking around free, much less holding seats in Congress.

Today's hearing was the crème de la crème. The Republican candidate for president was slated for questioning. Many claimed he had won the election, even with the landslide numbers Robert Murray had enjoyed. Rainey amused herself, imagining how many lawyers he'd bring along.

Patrick's phone was silent, but he received emails every few minutes. Most were from fans or donors, but he had a private address that picked up speed as the morning went on. Some from a Jet Prince with encrypted messages that N3Mo cracked in a matter of minutes. Messages about vehicles and his unit. Something was up, that much was certain.

On another screen were some texts from two senators about upcoming votes.

Senator Hines: *Today's the big day.*

Senator Babcock: *Yes, the hearing should be interesting.*

Hines: *That's not what I mean and you know it.*

Babcock: *Relax. And delete this thread.*

She read it again. Definitely something up.

Rainey checked her watch, then the Senate schedule. The hearing started at ten thirty. Two and a half hours. She went back to watching the militias make money.

The silence was punctuated by keyboard clicks, then Drake shouted, "Bingo!"

Rainey's head swiveled around. "What?"

He read, "'Frank Foley, a.k.a. Agent Gene Olson. Ex-Marine. Black ops in Iraq. Joined the Company in 2015. Now the leader of Patriot League.' Looks like they sent you after the wrong guy," Drake said.

"Was somebody assigned to him?" she asked.

Drake shrugged and clicked another file open. "Whoa, Nelly. Look at this."

*Mission: Infiltrate group. Fuel skepticism of government. Create distrust in the upcoming election. Encourage insurrectionist activity. Liaise with other operatives in similar groups. Report to Red Fox.*

"Who is Red Fox?" both Rainey and N3Mo asked at the same time.

"Well now, that is the question, isn't it?" Drake said.

"So which side is this guy working for?" N3Mo asked, his forehead wrinkled. Or what Rainey could see of his forehead.

"I don't know," Drake said. "Let's find out."

The two hackers went to work mining the intelligence agencies' data banks. Rainey made herself a cup of green tea and went back to her chair. She started watching the government screens. Still pretty quiet.

Suddenly, R's screen lit up.

"We've got a new drop," Rainey announced.

"Let us know if it's anything interesting," Drake mumbled.

>R !!TcQl7okW7o9/29/21 (Fri) 08:06:29 ID: 8e583d (5) No. 9458203>


>>2.00002

Awake? Locked and loaded?

R

Rainey read the drop to the two hackers, who only grunted in reply. She looked back at Jack Patrick's secret phone and sat up straighter. The thing was exploding.

Central: *Operation Roost commencing at 08:10. Report.*

Unit C: *Roger that.*

Unit A: *Roger.*

"We've got action." Rainey yelled to Drake.

Two more units responded. Four so far.

She picked up her cell and called Control. "Something's going down. Drake is sending the link."

The two hackers started tracing the signals.

Unit B: *15 to 15*

"What does that mean?" N3Mo asked.

"It means you show up fifteen minutes earlier than you're supposed to," Rainey explained.

"Why would anybody do that?" the teen asked.

"So you don't get chewed out by your unit commander for being three seconds late."

The teenager shook his head. At least it looked like he did. She could barely see him inside his hoodie. "I'm never joining," he muttered.

Rainey turned back up at the big display. Two red dots appeared on the big screen Drake had cleared to track this operation.

"That's their command near the Pentagon."

"Holy shit," N3Mo whispered.

"Buckle up, buttercup," Rainey whispered.

N3Mo was too engrossed to take offense.

Drake pointed at another dot just west of Arlington. "That's your boy, Patrick."

No more units had responded. "So we've got two mobiles and one command center?" Rainey asked.

"So far," Drake mumbled.

The two hackers hunched over their keyboards, clicking maniacally. In under thirty seconds, another dot appeared near Andrews Air Force Base. "Nick Rangel of Aryan Authority." The dot started moving toward the city.

She checked the Senate feed. "Nothing happening in the Capitol yet."

"Think this is related to the hearing?" Drake asked.

"Most likely, but what are they up to? They don't seem to be headed to the Hill."

Control burst through the door. "The feds are sending out people, but they could be compromised. Same with military command."

A fourth red dot appeared, this one heading to the northern suburbs.

"I thought we had more time. Why haven't they cleaned out Earl's appointees?" Control slammed his hand down on the table full of equipment in front of him. Equipment jiggled, then settled back.

"What are your orders, sir?" Rainey asked. She'd never seen him rattled. Her question focused him.

He turned to her and gave her a clipped nod, as if in thanks. "You're on Patrick. Follow him and report in. Don't intervene unless it looks like a principal's life is at stake."

Rainey headed for the door.

"I'll let you know who else I send out to cover the other mobile units."

"Roger that." She reached for the doorknob.

"Looks like we're on our own," she heard Control say just as the door swung shut.

# 8

G rant waited by the door of the limo parked in front of the home of the Speaker of the House of Representatives. He shifted his weight from one foot to the other, anxious about what they were doing. He was also pissed. Brad had ambushed him. He'd filled Grant in on the operation only an hour before it went live. Either Brad didn't care or didn't think the members of his group would have a problem being involved in treason of the highest order. Didn't give it a second thought. He said jump and Grant was supposed to ask how high. Period.

Brad had always been pushy, but ever since President Earl's death, something was off about him. He strutted around like he had something to prove. Bullied the new recruits something awful. Jumped at sudden noises.

Chatter came from the front walkway and Grant stood up straighter. Voices drifted to him, still too far away to understand words. He pulled at his suit again.

How had he'd gotten so deep so fast? He'd only met the general at the fundraiser. They'd never met in Afghanistan. Well, at a distance, but that didn't count. General Steve Keegan ran the whole show back in Kandahar. The man's name had popped to the surface of his memory like a corked bottle while Grant tossed and turned in his bed last night. Apparently, Keegan was in charge of this part of the operation.

There were other pieces of the plan happening simultaneously, but Grant didn't know where or what was involved. He wasn't on the need-to-know list. He didn't think Brad was either, although he bet the team lead was certain he knew it all. Grant glanced around to where his boss sat in the back of the vehicle, syringe ready.

"Eyes front, soldier," Brad snapped.

Grant turned back around and studied the flagstone walkway between the boxwood hedges. Today they'd paired with some trussed up cowboy named Jack Patrick. Brad said he was head of the Sons of Liberty. What happened to that guy they'd spied on the other night? Was Frank Foley his name with the so-called Patriot League? They all considered themselves patriots, as the names of their groups and their twitter hashtags showed, but Grant knew better.

What they were doing was treason, plain and simple. But General Keegan and Brad, along with all the other numb nuts who'd planned and were now executing Operation Save America, thought their targets were the traitors. Grant was just a pawn on the board, and it was getting too deep for him. He'd have to find a way out. Except he kept coming up with dead ends.

*Should've followed Derrick out the door.*

Grant spotted the Speaker of the House halfway down her walk. Too late now. He could yell out, let her know what was happening, but ten to one they'd both be dead five seconds after that. Shot. Two to the chest, one to the head. They'd put the weapon in Grant's lifeless hand and claim it had all been his idea.

So, that wouldn't work.

General Keegan walked with her, their heads together as they talked. She didn't have a clue. Her bodyguards walked behind her, eyes alert, but relaxed. They knew Keegan. So did she.

She paused when she spotted Grant, though.

*Good girl,* he thought.

"My goodness, lots of changes today."

"Yes, ma'am," Keegan said. "Like I said, we're on high alert. The Capitol Police and the FBI have noticed a lot of chatter about the hearing today."

The Speaker's gaze turned to Grant. "Then you won't mind me asking a question."

General Keegan nodded to him.

"Of course not. It's good practice," Grant said, though it had been years since he'd used the challenge and password. He thought about giving her the wrong answer, but then Keegan knew it. Everybody around him did. It would be the same as yelling out a warning with the exact same results.

"Did you eat *breakfast* this morning?" the Speaker asked.

Grant gulped, his mind suddenly blank. Brad had told him just this morning. What the hell was it?

Speaker Woods waited, one carefully groomed eyebrow raised. She was smaller than she appeared on television, really a sparrow of a woman, but she had the gaze of a raptor.

"Oh, sorry. I had toast with *apricot* jam."

With a nod, she entered the vehicle. General Keegan slid in behind her. Grant heard a cry of alarm.

Two shooters emerged from the vehicle behind them and took out the two bodyguards while they were still reaching for their weapons. One fell still trying to speak into the mic on his wrist, but the second gunman finished him off with a shot to the head.

Grant slid into the front passenger seat, his stomach a sick knot. The Speaker was slumped over. Out cold.

Brad carefully put the syringe back in its long plastic case.

"Let's go," the general said.

The driver pulled away from the curb and proceeded down the street, slow and easy, so they didn't attract any attention.

Brad threw the Speaker's phone to Grant. "Disable it."

Then he swept her briefcase, purse, and body for any bugs. "She's clean."

Grant bent the SIM card from her phone in half and threw it out the window, then rolled the window back up. The dark glass hid their crime.

After a few miles, the driver announced. "We've got company."

"Where?" Patrick asked.

"See that white sedan? I'm making a turn up here. Try to get a look at the driver."

Patrick pulled out a pair of field glasses and waited for a better view. Once they maneuvered around the intersection, the sedan pulled up to the light. He put the binoculars to his face. "I'll be goddamned. It's that same bitch."

"Who?" three people asked at once.

Patrick told the story of how some woman named Suzy had planted spyware on his phone. "I invited her to my house after dinner. She thought she would get more intel, but we jumped her."

Grant pulled the visor down and tried to get a glimpse of Patrick in the mirror on the back. All he could see was the nape of his neck.

"Bitch could fight, though. I wonder what agency she was from." He pointed at the general. "They couldn't find any record of her."

A chill went through Grant.

Brad must have been thinking the same thing. "What'd she looked like?"

"Medium height, well-muscled. Moved like a dancer. Skin the color of coffee with too much cream. Wore a blond wig, but had dark hair. Tried to pass herself off as white with a tan." Patrick said with disgust.

"Nah, it couldn't be." Brad almost whispered. "Not again."

Grant was thinking the same. Madison. The woman under Brad's command in Afghanistan. The woman they'd kidnapped and assaulted. The woman who he'd thought was dead until he saw her in Atlanta. She'd had the chance to shoot him, but hadn't done it. Instead, she let him take credit for killing the famous assassin, The Albanian, and walked away. Was Madison here?

RAINEY PUSHED the white Ford Crown Victoria she'd commandeered faster down Route 123. She activated her com. "Home 2, this is Alpha: Looks like they've got Pamela Woods."

"This is Home 2: They kidnapped the Speaker of the House?" Drake sounded incredulous.

"I didn't have eyes on, but they stopped at her address. Now they're headed out."

"But you're not sure."

Rainey blew out a breath. "Just try to contact her."

As Rainey waited to hear back from Drake, she merged onto the George Washington Memorial Parkway. She reported her location, although she was sure the group was tracking her.

A minute later, Control's voice came through her com. "The police reported two Secret Service agents dead outside the Speaker's house. Nobody can locate her."

"Are they keeping it from the media?"

"So far, but some rookie got on his scanner to talk."

"Damn. That's all we need. Reporters swarming. Public panic."

"Right. Stay on Patrick."

"Roger that."

Rainey positioned her Crown Vic just out of sight of the Escalade limo carrying the Speaker. At least she hoped the woman was in it. Rainey admired Speaker Woods. As a young woman, she'd gone into politics in the seventies, working her way up by serving state, then federal office holders. In the early eighties, she'd run for state office and won, then been elected to the House of Representatives where she'd been for twenty years.

Rainey knew what it was like to work with mostly men. A lot of them were decent and respectful, but there were always plenty who looked to take advantage or just unconsciously dismissed her ideas. Woods had persevered, maintaining her poise and her progressive politics. Now she was fighting to get to the bottom of the insurrection attempt, undeterred by daily vile threats. Rainey would be damned if she let this woman come to harm.

She punched her com again. "Any news on the other units?"

"We've identified the unit headed into the city as the Aryan Authority. We weren't able to establish surveillance on Nick Rangel's phone, but looks like they're headed for Georgetown."

Rainey didn't ask how they were tracking him. Patrick's convoy exited the parkway and headed toward the city. She followed, catching a glimpse of the group of black SUVs as they curved around the cloverleaf. When they reached the street, two police motorcycles took the lead, turning on their sirens and taking Patrick through red lights. Rainey was left in their wake.

"Patrick got a police escort."

"Let me check," Drake said.

Rainey wove through D.C. traffic, dodging slow cars and taxis pulling to pick people up, leaving a few honking horns and people shaking their fists. Not cool to draw attention to herself.

"No orders on record for a police escort," Drake reported.

Rainey doubled her speed. The Crown Vic handled like a tank. Why didn't it have a siren? Wasn't this the car all the police drove?

A man in a blue suit paused in the crosswalk, arguing on his phone. A bus blocked Rainey's way around him on the right, and oncoming traffic prevented her from swerving into the wrong lane. He stood there, waving his arms. Entitled little prick. She blew her horn and he shot her a look. Somebody behind her blew their horn as well, so he started to move. Rainey floored it and the vehicle answered her. But on the other side of the intersection, a family had moved off the curb.

She glanced at her phone. Now Patrick's dot was six blocks ahead. Two others blinked in residential neighborhoods. She didn't have time to ask Drake whose houses they were.

She zipped around the family, raising a yell from the mother who pushed her stroller faster. Patrick's dot now blinked close to a mile ahead of her. She would catch up eventually. Unless he headed for the airport, but the dot traveled west in the general direction of the National Cathedral. At least the traffic would slow him down, too.

Her progress improved as she blended with traffic. She laughed. Master Chu, her martial arts instructor, often chided her to relax.

That hurrying always slowed things down. As she gained on the dot, the neighborhood changed from art galleries, coffee shops, and various boutiques to apartment houses that had seen better days. Gusts of wind picked up trash on the street and blew it around in lazy puffs.

The red dot stopped. She was within half a mile of her target. The buildings had moved from down-at-heel apartments to ramshackle garages and a few liquor stores, each with a row of men sitting outside holding paper bags, their tops folded back. Dilapidated warehouses replaced these, many with broken or boarded-up windows.

Three blocks away from Patrick's location, she turned into a parking lot that sported weeds breaking through the concrete and pulled up Google maps. The satellite view of the area showed empty brick buildings and alleys filled with trash and a few abandoned shopping carts. Patrick seemed to be parked in a small turn-out next to a creek. A metal fence blocked off the water—or what was left of it. The backs of the buildings running along this dirt road had no windows. Rainey spotted an opening between an old metal shop and garage close to Patrick's vehicle.

Rainey parked her Crown Vic behind an overflowing dumpster and carried her Glock 19 in her right hand down against her leg. She took a deep breath and stretched her awareness out to harmonize with her surroundings. Two rats feasting on something she didn't want to look at too closely sniffed at her from the other side of the alley, their whiskers moving with their nose, then turned back to their meal.

Rainey moved silently to the end of the alley and spotted the car a block down. She waited, listening for any sound, alert for movement. The black limo sat quiet, engine off, doors closed. A skinny dog with swollen teats came up from the creek through a hole in the fence and sniffed around the vehicle.

No doors opened. No voices shouted. No response at all.

Rainey walked closer, spotting two sets of tire tracks in the dust that headed down the dirt road away from the Escalade. She reached the car and tried the back door. It opened. Papers were strewn over the back seat. She slipped on a thin latex glove and picked one up. The letterhead read, 'Speaker of the House.'

Rainey backed out of the car and looked around, but the alley was empty. She reached for her phone and hit Control's burner for the day.

"Yes?"

"Pamela Woods has been kidnapped. Vehicle abandoned. No security cams around."

He let out a heavy breath. "Roger that. I'll send out a team."

Rainey snapped pictures of the interior of the limo and closeups of the tire tracks. She needed to hurry before the evidence team arrived. She did a second sweep of the back, then started on the front. Patrick's phone sat on the seat, glowing. She leaned over and looked at the screen.

*Bitch.*

Damn it. She thought she'd been so careful.

Something caught her eye on the floorboard. A scrap of paper with something scribbled on it. She picked it up. A logo at the top was torn in half, but enough was left for her to recognize it.

Red Sky.

Rainey's stomach clinched. Was it Brad Rogers' unit? Would she ever be rid of him?

A phone number was scrawled across the bottom, a few tiny holes in the paper suggested someone had written on it with no firm backing. Or they were in a big hurry and used too much force.

Red Sky. The group had been in Atlanta. Private security for former President Earl. She'd run into them again at Ibis Isle, Earl's private retreat, where her unexpected ally had taken care of Brad, the leader of the gang who'd raped her. This note couldn't be from him. After his humiliation in the Florida Keys, he would be out to get her. Maybe he wrote the little explicative, although she thought it more likely that it was Patrick.

Then she remembered Grant Mendez standing there with his mouth hanging open in Atlanta, telling her she was supposed to be dead. Could Grant be mixed up in all this? Could he finally be having second thoughts about following Brad around and doing his bidding?

Rainey pocketed the note and closed the car doors. The dog sat nearby, looking at her with hopeful eyes. She wished she had something to give her. Rainey smiled, remembering the well-meaning therapist who'd suggested she get a puppy. Not with her lifestyle. She couldn't even keep a teapot.

Rainey approached the scruffy canine, eyes low. The dog froze, then sniffed Rainey's offered hand. She ran her hand over the dog's head, giving her a blessing, then jogged back to her vehicle. She'd come back later with some food for the little family when she could.

## 9

Rainey slowed to a walk so she wouldn't draw attention, although the neighborhood seemed empty. She activated her com. "I'm heading out."

"Alpha, this is Home 2," Drake said, using the formal group reporting protocol. "Switch to Channel 5. All units coordinating."

Rainey clicked to the proper channel. "Alpha here."

"Net call," Drake said, addressing everyone on the net, "this is Home 2: Report."

"Home 2, this is Alpha. I'm done here. What's happening?"

"Alpha, this is Home 1." *Weird.* She didn't expect Control to be coordinating for this operation. He was more of a behind the scenes guy. "Other tails report the same switch. Dilapidated neighborhood with no security cameras all over town."

"Home 1, you're running this op?" she asked.

His chuckle was as smooth as expensive Scotch whisky. "All hands on deck."

She laughed. "I thought it was something about every swinging—"

"Let's focus, shall we?"

"Do we have any of them on the board?"

"Home 2 is in Foley's phone."

"Great." Control's use of these codes further reminded her they were operational.

"Net call, this is Delta. We have eyes on the Aryan Authority."

"Delta, this is Home 2: Where are they headed?"

"South on the George Washington Memorial Parkway. We just passed Alexandria."

"This is Alpha: I'm on the way."

"Alpha, this is Home 1: Roger that."

Rainey wove her way to the fastest route south, jumping onto the parkway within five minutes. She listened to the feed from the op.

"Home 1, this is Delta. Still headed south. Any suspicious activity down there?"

"This is Home 1: Checking now."

Rainey listened to the crackling of the electronic feed. She checked her radar. No state patrol around. They'd probably been called in to help with the kidnappings. She pushed the Crown Vic to 100 mph. The car started to shake, so she backed off to 95.

Her eyes darted to her phone in the passenger seat. Three red dots traveled south. Their team marked with blue dots followed, one so close it blurred with the targets. She reached over and expanded the view. The dots separated, showing a good half mile between the kidnapper and pursuer.

The feed crackled again.

"Net call, this is Home 1: We've got another drop."

The message swam up on Rainey's phone. She picked it up and read, glancing between the screen and the road.

>R !!TcQl7okW709/29/21 (Fri) 08:06:29 ID: 8e583d (5) No. 9458203>


>>2.00003

Charge!

R

*Shit!* Rainey gunned the engine.

"This is Home 1: National Park Service is reporting people converging on Mount Vernon. They called for help."

"Home 1, this is Bravo: Aryan Authority close to Mount Vernon."

"Bravo, this is Home 1: Roger that."

*Mount Vernon? What the hell?* Rainey pushed the sedan up past 100 mph again, clamping down on the wheel to control the shimmy.

---

MOANS ISSUED from the backseat of the Escalade. Grant steeled himself not to turn around. Brad hadn't told him what they were going to do once they kidnapped Speaker Woods. He'd just muttered, "It's need to know and you don't."

It looked to Grant like they were heading to Mount Vernon. He couldn't for the life of him imagine why. Traffic had picked up, too. After they crossed the bridge, he noticed a lot of older cars and trucks with bumper stickers sporting right-wing slogans.

*Where is Earl?*

*You will not replace us.*

*Keep the country Christian.*

Grant heard movement. It was the speaker struggling to sit up. "What's happening?" she asked, her words muddled from the drug.

Grant lowered the visor and pulled up the flap over the mirror. He had to see if she was all right.

Speaker Woods rubbed her face with her two hands, then tried to reach for her purse, but the zip-ties stopped her. Her eyes flew wide. "Why are my hands tied? What's going on?"

Nobody answered her.

The sedative was wearing off more and more. She pointed at Brad, who was sitting in the seat directly across from her, facing the rear of the vehicle. "Where is General Keegan?" she demanded, her voice stronger now.

"Right beside you."

Speaker Woods turned toward him and stared in disbelief. "What are you doing? You'll be court martialed for this."

"Now Pamela, you didn't think we'd let you question Brian Hoffman, did you? And bring charges against those patriotic senators who helped when we tried to take the country back?"

Speaker Woods stared at him, open-mouthed, momentarily speechless.

In the stop and go traffic, people were leaning out of their cars yelling. One bald man rolled down his window and screamed at the Escalade, his face deep red, "Hang them all."

"Death to traitors," someone in a truck behind him shouted back, their voices somehow penetrating the bullet-proof windows.

Grant's whole body froze. He stared at the dash in front of him. Surely this was just more bravado, but then the limo stopped. Trucks sat willy-nilly in front of the main entrance to Mount Vernon. Two large cabs from semi-trucks blocked the gate.

General Keegan rolled down the window and shouted orders. "Clear these vehicles out."

The man in charge jumped to attention, surprised by the general's sudden appearance. "Yes, sir."

Engines fired up and the vehicles backed away, making a path. An ancient Chevy Impala tried to push through, but two men blocked the way, one pounding on the hood, the other pointing an AR-15 at the driver.

Speaker Woods reached out and laid her hands on General Keegan's arm. "You can't do this, Steve. This is insane."

He jerked his arm away. "Is it? I'll tell you what's insane. Having President Earl assassinated so you could take over the government."

"We didn't have anything—" Speaker Woods started to say, but General Keegan ran right over her objection.

"You're giving the country away, Pamela. All that money for people too lazy to work. Taxing corporations so much they'll flee the country. All these faggots running around and we have to let them serve. And who knows what anybody is anymore. Man. Woman. Now anybody can be a man. All they have to do is just say they feel like one."

"General Keegan!" Speaker Woods said, her voice sharp, used to command, but he still ignored her.

"To say nothing of immigrants. The United States of America was founded by white Christian men and look around you. A sea of black and brown faces."

Grant looked into the mirror again. General Keegan was leaning over the speaker, snarling. Something deep shifted in Grant. He suppressed a flood of rage. He couldn't give anything away, but he had to find a way to save Pamela Woods. Grant wouldn't let these monsters kill another woman.

The speaker recovered a little. "I would never have pegged you for a white supremacist, Steve. But we can talk about all this."

"I hid it well, didn't I? What choice did you give me?"

The car stopped. "We're here, sir."

"The time for debate is long past. Now is the time for action," Keegan said.

———

RAINEY DODGED the growing traffic as she got closer to Mount Vernon. She listened to the com information carefully.

"Net call, this is Home 1: Mount Vernon police report National Park personnel locked into Texas Gate office. Multiple 911 calls. Workers and tourists herded into buildings by men and women with guns."

The line exploded with questions.

"... type of gun?"

"... uniforms?"

"Net call, this is Home 1: Quiet."

Rainey woke up her phone. All three red dots had crossed the Potomac and were headed straight for George Washington's estate. Two blue dots followed close on their heels.

"This is Home 1: Crowd gathered on the lawn near the mansion. Sounds of hammering."

"Hammering?" Rainey blurted out.

"Roger that. Multiple police units responding."

"They've called in the National Guard, but I don't think they'll get there in time."

"This is Home 2: All ground units, move in. Blend with the crowd."

Grumbling came over the coms. Then a clear voice, "Home 2, this is Bravo. Sir, with respect. We're in tactical dress."

"These are fucking militias. Blend in."

Rainey had never heard Control curse before. She took the bridge at 110 mph, weaving around slower traffic. Horns blared and some middle fingers appeared from rolled down windows. She pushed the sedan to 125 mph, manhandling the car through the shaking, then slowed within a quarter mile of the gate.

Abandoned cars littered the sides of the road. Up ahead, a knot of vehicles blocked the road. Rainey grabbed her Steiner binoculars. She could make out four large pickups and two cabs from semi-trucks clogging the entrance to the park. She found an opening in the abandoned vehicles and nosed the sedan into it. The rear stuck out, but she didn't have time to straighten up. Rainey grabbed her assault pack and headed for a stand of sycamore trees.

Nobody noticed her as she ran across a small field. They were all headed for the mansion. She ducked into the woods and started to make her way toward the knot of people in the emerald stretch of lawn in front of the white columned colonial crowning the hill.

Squinting her eyes against the bright October sun, she saw new yellow wood held up by a crowd of people. A man climbed a ladder and started nailing a piece to another slat.

*What the hell?*

As she got closer, snippets of conversation drifted to her.

". . . traitors. We won't put up with them no more."

"Think they can interrogate the rightful president of America."

She crouched behind a winterberry bush still hung with red berries. The two men stood a few feet away, talking to each other. One wore a brown plaid flannel shirt that almost matched his hair and full beard. He carried a Ruger hunting rifle.

His companion wore fatigues, but Rainey couldn't make out the unit patch from the back. The barrel of an M-4 stuck out from over his left elbow. Must be active military.

The first man turned his head and spit a stream of tobacco juice. "They here yet?"

The second pushed the button on his radio. "ETA?"

"Pulling in now."

"How long you reckon we need to stay here?" the first man asked. "I want to see them swing, especially that bitch Woods."

"We're on duty, soldier," the real soldier said.

The first man dug the toe of his boot into the pine needles like a scolded child. "I suppose."

*Swing? Fuck, they're going to hang them,* Rainey thought.

That explained the hammering. These nut jobs were building a scaffold just like they'd done at the Capitol. But this time, they were putting up more than one, and their intended victims were in custody.

A roar went up from the crowd closer to the road. Rainey pulled back from behind the winterberry bush and followed a deer track toward the lawn. A crowd stood craning their necks and pushing forward to see what was happening up front. Rainey stuffed an old Earl campaign hat on her head and moved out from cover. Nobody in the crowd noticed her joining them.

She turned on the photo option on her cell phone and held it over the heads of the people in front of her. The camera revealed three toughs pushing a man in a blue suit with a hood over his head in front of them. He stumbled, but they caught him. They pulled the hood off and Alan David, Majority Leader of the Senate, stood blinking in the sun.

"Hang him," came a few shouts from the crowd.

Rainey pulled her phone to her ear while activating her com. "You seeing this?" She tried to inject glee into her voice.

"Roger that."

Police sirens sounded from a distance.

Another group of men pushed another suited man through the

crowd. They pulled his hood off and Senator Todd Stein, head of the Judiciary Committee, glared at them.

The ambient noise changed, and it took Rainey a moment to realize the hammering had stopped. The crowd surged forward, giving Rainey a view at last. On the knoll stood three gallows.

Rainey had to do something fast. She didn't know where the other agents were in the crowd and even if she could find them, they were vastly outnumbered. An idea formed. She pulled the scrap of paper she'd found at the bottom of the Escalade and texted a message.

*You left this number for me in the limo.*

She hoped whoever was on the other end was a friend and not a foe.

# 10

Two men with Sig pistols appeared outside the speaker's side of the limo. Brad slid across the seat and opened the general's door. General Keegan got out and straightened his uniform.

Brad grabbed Speaker Woods and pushed her across the seat. Her shoe caught on something on the floorboard. She twisted, tried to catch herself, but her hands were still bound.

"Careful, you'll hurt her," Grant said before he could stop himself.

"That's exactly what we plan to do, moron," Brad sneered.

Brad pulled Speaker Woods out by her arm, but she got her feet under her and stood proud, defiant.

The crowd roared. Some took up a chant, "Hang them all." Others repeated it and soon it spread, a drumbeat of voices.

Grant felt a vibration in his pocket. It took him a minute to realize it was his personal cellphone. The open back door of the vehicle shielded him from the others. He pulled the phone out and read the message.

*You left this number for me in the limo.*
*Help! They're going to kill her.*
*Who is this?*

*Grant. Is this Madison?*

There was a long pause at the other end. The typing bubble started, then stopped, then started again. Finally, *Let's not get side-tracked. Where are you?*

*I'm with Speaker Woods.*

*You have to save her.*

*Where are you?*

*Coming.*

Brad pushed Speaker Woods over to stand beside her two compatriots. A man cut her hands free. She ran a few steps, but vigilantes circled the group. Two caught her and tossed her back and forth between them, laughing.

"Not so tough now, are you?" one said.

"We'll show you how we deal with traitors."

"That's enough." Brad intervened and dragged Speaker Woods back to the line. Her jacket was torn on one side from the rough handling. A soldier pulled her hands behind her and zip-tied them again. Other soldiers did the same to Representative Stein and Majority Leader David.

Grant stared. The men wore their dress uniforms as if they were showing up for some formal occasion. Traitorous bastards.

General Keegan mounted the gallows that stood in the middle of the three structures and took up a bullhorn. "Patriots!" he shouted, but the crowd just kept chanting.

He raised his hands for quiet. A few people stopped, but most were too caught up in the frenzy.

He tried again. "Friends, patriots, countrymen, listen to me."

He had prepared a speech, Grant realized in disgust. As the crowd settled down, police sirens in the distance replaced their chant. He prayed they'd get here in time.

General Keegan looked back toward the road and then nodded to a group of his men. Their platoon leader gave a clipped salute and mouthed an order Grant couldn't hear. The group headed off toward the road.

These assholes were going to shoot at the cops. Then he remembered they'd killed one at the attempted insurrection, so he shouldn't be surprised. Grant looked around him, desperate for an idea to stop this madness.

Keegan put the bullhorn to his mouth. "Here we have the Majority Leader of the Senate, Alan David."

The crowd erupted in boos and screamed insults.

"This man—" two men pushed Senator David up the stairs of the first gallows "—refused to investigate the assassination of President Earl. Instead, he swore in the imposter. How do you judge him?"

"Guilty," shouted several men in the front. The crowd took up the chant.

Keegan raised his left hand for quiet and spoke into the megaphone. "What should we do?"

"Hang him. Hang him," shouted the crowd.

The insurgents pushed the senator onto a narrow plank laying across an opening below the crossbar of the gallows. A man dressed in an old-fashioned hangman's outfit put a thick noose around Senator David's head.

*Oh, shit.* Grant's hand went to his weapon.

But the mercenaries didn't knock the wood out from under the senator.

Grant pulled his sidearm and moved toward the mercenaries holding Speaker Woods.

The wail of police sirens grew louder.

Keegan pointed at the next man in line beside the speaker. "This man is head of the Judiciary Committee that is trying all the good patriots that attempted to stop the fake election from going through."

"He's the traitor," a man in the crowd close to Grant shouted.

Gunfire sounded from near the gate to the property.

Grant moved forward, using the car as cover. He knew chances were good he'd get killed, but he had to act.

"Representative Stein thinks he can judge us," General Keegan continued.

Grant got a glimpse of Keegan's face when the man turned in his direction. It was red as a chili pepper.

A few shouts of "You will not replace us" rang out.

Grant frowned, confused by that one, until he remembered that Stein was probably a Jewish name.

Gunfire erupted again, this time closer than before, but Grant kept his focus on the men holding Speaker Woods.

The two men holding Representative Stein frog-marched him up the gallows, subduing his struggles. The hangman slipped the noose around his neck. Once again, they didn't kick the plank out from under his feet.

Looked like they wanted to let them all swing together. Grant still had time to do something. If he had a different weapon, he could shoot the ropes in two. He'd been practicing.

Keegan pointed at Speaker Woods.

Brad and his partner pushed her toward the third gallows, but the crowd had gotten thick.

Police swarmed in from the mansion, soldiers and armed civilians firing. Some engaged in hand-to-hand combat. A battle raged on the lawn.

Helicopter blades made a whup, whup, coming in from the west.

Brad looked up, shielding his eyes.

Grant glanced up as well, but then heard a cry of surprise. A figure in black fatigues jumped on the first gallows and punched a man on the platform holding the majority leader. He fell.

The other two men attacked, but the small figure responded with a blur of punches and kicks.

Grant recognized her. The woman he'd watched get killed in Afghanistan without doing a thing to help her. But she'd come back from the dead. Somehow.

He knew Pamela Woods would not come back from the dead. He wasn't about to make the same mistake again.

Brad turned to Grant and pointed at the figure on the gallows. "Shoot that bitch," he screamed. So Brad had recognized her too.

CROUCHED DOWN, Rainey waited for the next attack, but it didn't come. Three men lay sprawled around her. She stood and walked up behind the Majority Leader, steadying him with a hand on his shoulder. Reaching into a pouch on her thigh, she pulled out her Emerson tactical knife and cut the man's hands free.

"Oh, my God. Thank you." He started to turn around.

"Hold still. We're not done yet." She reached up with her right hand and loosened the knot on the rope, then pulled the noose over Senator David's head.

"Step back. Careful now." She guided him to the firm planks, away from the gap in the platform that had been meant for his swinging body.

"Stay behind me," she said.

"Gladly."

She surveyed the battle surging around her. Two men fought off the soldiers holding Representative Stein on the middle gallows. She squinted in the late morning sun and thought she could make out Andy and Theo. More hostiles swarmed toward the steps of that platform. They needed help, but Rainey's first priority was to guard the majority leader. She searched the crowd for friendlies.

A man in a nice suit hoisted himself up onto the platform. Gaining his feet, he pulled his Sig duty pistol. "Step away from the senator."

"She saved my life, Wayne."

Another man dressed in an identical suit ran up the platform, somehow not slipping in his black Italian oxfords. He started to raise his pistol, but stopped when he heard the senator.

"You guys got him?" Rainey asked.

"Yes, ma'am."

"Thank you for your—" the senator started, but Rainey ran down the steps of the gallows and headed toward the middle structure, the rest of the senator's words lost.

Three men dressed in jeans and work shirts stepped in front of her. "What do we have here?" said the one in blue plaid.

"What's this little nigger doing here?" The second man balled up his fist and pulled it back to hit her.

Ridiculously slow, Rainey thought. The man's stomach protruded from the straining buttons on his green shirt. Rainey planted a kick into it.

He flew back.

"Shit. The little bitch can—"

Rainey clocked blue plaid with a roundhouse punch, then knocked the third one in the temple. Both fell at her feet.

"Nice work, Suzy."

Rainey looked up to see Andy leering down at her. "Is Representative Stein secure?"

"You betcha."

Rainey shook her head. Moron to the last. She looked around for Speaker Woods and spotted her being pushed away from the limo toward the third gallows. Rainey ran toward her.

Suddenly, Grant stepped out with his pistol drawn. He waved it wildly at the crowd near the speaker.

*What the hell?*

---

GRANT TOOK A DEEP BREATH. It was time to stop this madness. Time to stand up to Brad.

"Stop!" he yelled, walking towards the gallows, outnumbered. If he could only make them see what a horrible mistake they're making, "You're pissed off," Grant yelled to the crowd. "I get that. You feel like you've been treated wrong. Like your country doesn't give a shit about you because you're strong enough to stand on your own two feet. But this—" he motioned toward the politicians, their eyes pleading for salvation "—this is not the way."

"What the hell are you doing?" Brad yelled.

The crowd was silent, their mouths agape.

"Putting a stop to this," Grant said, pulling Speaker Woods away from the men holding her.

He heard the slide of Brad's pistol racking back, chambering a round, and turned to face him.

"Step away from the speaker. We're here to execute these traitors. The people have spoken." Brad waved his gun toward the crowd.

People in the front ducked. A woman screamed.

Grant pushed Speaker Woods behind him. "I won't let you kill another woman like this."

Brad pointed his Makarov pistol at Grant. "I said step away from the prisoner." He spoke through gritted teeth.

Grant spread his arms. "You're gonna have to kill me first, brother."

---

ON THE SLIGHT rise ahead of her, Rainey saw Grant with Speaker Woods behind him, his arms spread, Brad pointing a gun at him.

*Jesus, what is he doing?* Rainey thought.

She waded into the melee of civilians and police, ducking several batons aimed at her head. She threw one man into a police officer, taking them both down. She cleared a way to top of the rise, kicking and punching.

Rainey heard the sirens in the distance, the faint whump whump whump of a helicopter. "What's the ETA?"

"Thirty seconds," Drake said.

So close, she saw the break in the gathered mass and maneuvered into position.

Over the growing whispers, she heard Grant say, "You're gonna have to kill me first, brother."

"So be it," Brad said, taking aim.

She owed Grant nothing, but here he was, doing the right thing. Finally. She couldn't just let him die.

Rainey stepped into view, her Glock 19 aimed at Brad. "Remember me?"

The sound of helicopter blades drew their attention.

Brad glanced wildly around at the lowering Black Hawk, then back at Rainey and Grant. He settled on Grant as his first target.

But Grant had leveled his pistol and already had him square in his sights.

Brad's eyes flew wide.

A squad of police ran toward them, guns drawn. "Step away from the speaker."

Brad pointed his weapon at Speaker Woods. "Death to traitors," he yelled.

But before he could get a round off, Grant fired.

Brad grabbed his chest, his mouth gaping open, shocked.

Grant glared down the sights, weapon held firm like a man hell bent on seeing this through. He pulled the trigger, the bullet aimed for Brad's forehead.

Brad Rogers fell dead at the speaker's feet.

Rainey bent down to make sure he was dead. Her rational mind told her he was. He'd taken two bullets to the chest and a bloody hole decorated his forehead. But she had to be certain he was gone. The man who'd haunted her dreams, destroyed her life, exiled her from her family. She felt for a pulse, but found none.

He lay dead at her feet. Finally.

A shadow fell over her and she looked up to see Grant staring at Brad, his gun still pointed.

And one of the men who should have protected her, but stood by and watched, had killed him. Tears filled her eyes. But Grant was still a live wire. Rainey stood up slowly, spreading her arms out. "Easy now," she said.

Grant blinked and focused on her. "I couldn't make the same mistake again."

Rainey moved beside him and put her hand on his shoulder. "Of course not."

"I couldn't let him kill her."

She reached for his pistol with her other hand. "He's not going to hurt anybody anymore."

Grant looked at her, his eyes swimming with tears. "I'm sorry."

"Give me the gun. You don't want the police to mistake you for an assassin."

Grant blinked, then said, "No, I guess that's your job."

Rainey gave a startled laugh. "Where's Speaker Woods?"

"Behind me." Grant gestured with his pistol.

"Drop your weapon," Two police officers shouted. They stood in front of them, guns aimed.

"But I—" Grant said.

"Drop your weapon or I'll fire."

Rainey raised her hands in the air. "Grant, drop the gun."

The confused man let the Makarov fall from his fingers.

"Kick it over here."

Grant stared, still stunned by the turn of events. Rainey kicked his pistol toward the officers.

"Hands behind your back."

"It's all right, officer," came a familiar voice. "He saved my life."

Speaker Woods walked up to Grant and extended her hand. "Thank you for your help in the end. What changed your mind?"

Grant's eyes filled. He cleared his throat and answered, "My commander kept getting me into bad situations." He tilted his head toward Brad.

"He was your commander?"

Grant stood a little straighter. "Yes, ma'am."

"You decided not to obey an unlawful order?"

He looked up at the speaker, confusion written on his face. One tear traced a silver track down his cheek. "I decided not to let him kill you."

"I am very grateful that you stopped him." Speaker Woods started to say more, but the roar of helicopter blades drowned out her voice.

A Black Hawk hovered over the field, slowly lowering down. They must be trying to scatter the crowd, Rainey thought. A few people with rifles and one with what looked like an AR-15 fired at the craft. Menacing black rifle barrels emerged from the crew compartment of the helicopter and soldiers returned fire, picking off two civilians who'd shot at them.

Another Black Hawk hung near the trees at the end of the lawn. Lines dropped from the belly of the machine and soldiers repelled down. The black barrels of MK-14 Enhanced Battle Rifles protruded from the belly of the machine, giving cover. At least that's what they used when Rainey had been in the service.

A squadron of National Guardsmen swarmed in from the tree line, mowing down anyone firing at them. They started corralling the unarmed domestic terrorists.

Nearby, a gruff voice rang out over the general clamor. "General Steve Keegan, you are under arrest. You have the right to remain silent."

"I will never be silenced," Keegan shouted.

The rest of his Miranda rights were drowned out by his loud protests. The police led him to a waiting MP and handed him off. The MP guided the general into the back of his vehicle, putting a hand on his head, observing all the correct protocol while the general screamed, "I am your superior officer. I order you to release me."

Behind them sat another patrol car with Jack Patrick in the back. He raised his shackled hands, pointed his index finger at Rainey, and mouthed what looked like, "Pow."

*Creep,* Rainey thought. He'd be in jail for a good while. At least, she hoped so.

One of the policemen surrounding the speaker spoke up, drawing Rainey's attention back. "Excuse me, Madam Speaker, but I'm afraid we'll have to take Mr. Mendez into custody for questioning."

"Of course, but I want to hear what happens to him." She looked around for something, then shook her head. "I was going to give you a private number for my office, but I seem to have lost my briefcase."

"We have it," Rainey said before she thought better of it.

"And who are you, may I ask?"

Rainey gave a little shake of her head. "We'll return it."

A policeman listened to his earpiece, then nodded at Rainey. "You're free to go."

She turned to leave.

"Who should I thank—" the speaker began, but Rainey had already moved into the crowd, disappearing from Pamela Woods' view.

She made her way across the field, nodding at soldiers as she went. Her tactical clothing and gear seemed to give her a free pass.

# 11

Rainey reached her white sedan and slid into the driver's seat. The burner phone she'd used as a decoy lay on the seat next to her, but she activated her com instead.

"Home 1, this is Alpha: All principals are safe. Hostiles contained."

"This is Home 1: Roger that."

"I'm taking a vacation."

She heard chuckles on the com.

"This is Home 1. Alpha, report back to—"

Rainey pulled the device out of her ear and threw it on the passenger seat next to the burner. She reached into her pack on the floorboard and found her personal phone. Arnold's number sat at the top of her list. She tapped it to send a message.

*Coming to visit if u r available.*

In a few seconds, the phone dinged.

*Looking forward to it.*

Rainey turned the car around and headed to the highway. She drove in silence, letting the surges of adrenaline subside. The nightmare Brad Rogers had started in Afghanistan was over, but she still couldn't go back to her old life. She'd been irrevocably changed. She could never see her family again. Sail with her father. Make Jamaican Jerk chicken with her mother—although she'd stopped eating chicken.

But some good had come of it, she supposed. She had a new family of Buddhist nuns in Tibet. The head of their order approved of her divine mission to clear out what the ancient woman called 'demons' from the world. They were just bad men in Rainey's view. Who knows how they'd become evil, but they'd get a new chance with a new life. And she'd met Arnold. She smiled and switched on her favorite playlist.

As she approached the city, the face of the mother dog who'd turned up next to the speaker's abandoned car swam up in her memory. She'd promised. Rainey took an exit when she saw a shopping center and found a grocery store. She bought two packets of ground chicken and traced her way through the back streets of D.C. to the site.

The dusty road sat empty now. The crime scene had been cleared, the mystery solved. Rainey got out of her car and retrieved her grocery bag. She tore open a packet of meat and placed it on the road about five feet away. The other she kept next to her. Rainey leaned against a fence post, listening for the dog. The canine would be scared from all the recent activity.

After about ten minutes, Rainey decided to meditate. She sat cross-legged on the yellowed grass. It took her a while to settle into silence after the excitement of the day. Images of the battle kept bursting up from her memory, her body sometimes jerking in response. Eventually, Rainey dropped into a restful quiet.

A few minutes later, she heard the dog approach. Rainey stayed still, eyes closed, still meditating. The dog began to eat. Rainey opened her eyes and watched. Under the dirt covering the dog's coat, Rainey saw a bit of yellow. A lab maybe. Perhaps a golden retriever, but she didn't seem big enough. Still, malnourishment would have stunted her growth.

The dog finished her meal, then approached Rainey, stiff-legged. Her nostrils flared as she sniffed out the second packet of chicken.

Hunger won out over fear. She approached, growling low to let Rainey know she was prepared to defend herself.

Rainey remained still. The dog reached for the packet of meat, then jumped back, unsure. Rainey started a quiet hum. The dog tilted her head, ears perked. Rainey opened the packet of chicken and offered her a handful. The dog grabbed it and pulled back to chew.

Rainey offered her another handful. The dog's tail wagged tentatively.

"It's all right. You can eat."

*What am I doing?* she wondered. *I can't take her with me.*

Or could she?

Little yips sounded from the ditch. The grass waved with movement. Soon, three small heads peered out from the weeds. Two yellow faces and one black. The puppy's mother heaved a huge sigh and laid down next to Rainey. The little ones took this as a sign that all was safe and came wiggling toward her. They seemed to be about four weeks old. Rainey opened the second packet of chicken and the puppies devoured it, then settled against their mother to nurse.

Rainey got to her feet, preparing to leave.

The mother dog looked at her, eyes begging.

"Oh, hell," she mumbled.

What would Arnold say? She'd already brought a stray kitten to The Oaks. Iset would be pretty big by now.

"You can't chase the cat," she said.

The dog thumped her tail as if in agreement.

"Come on, then." The dog followed her to the Crown Vic.

Rainey stripped off her sweatshirt and found an old t-shirt in her gym bag. She made a little bed in the back seat, then moved aside. The dog jumped in. The puppies bounced on their hind legs, trying to follow, but couldn't manage the height. Rainey picked them up and deposited them next to their mother. She'd have to get a bowl for water.

Rainey got into the front, started car, and headed north, no longer alone.

FROM HIS OFFICE IN RUSSIA, Esen Ahmad reviewed the feed of the attempted hanging of the three top leaders of the U.S. Congress from his plant's body cam. These Americans loved a good lynching.

The crowd had failed in the assassination attempt, but he didn't really care about that. The deaths of the leaders were not vital to the overall plan. His group had succeeded in planting permanent doubts in the minds of a good third of the American public about their government and its agencies, not to mention their election process. More importantly, they'd been stirred to take treasonous action against their rulers. Excellent progress that would serve the cabal in their next operation. The A-2 conspiracy group was solid and he could count on them to undermine their colleagues in governments from local all the way up to the U.S. Capitol.

Esen patted the manila envelope he'd gotten from Kiselev, then stored it in his wall safe. If this mysterious assassin showed up again, he had her file. The next time, they would eliminate her.

WANT to know when Rainey takes on her next target? Join my newsletter to hear about new releases, special offers, and news. Click here to subscribe. No spam and it's easy to unsubscribe.

REVIEWS HELP WRITERS KEEP WRITING. Please feel free to leave one!

# ABOUT THE AUTHOR

T.L. Crater writes thrillers with a mystical twist.

# ALSO BY

**T.L. Crater**

Mystic Assassin Series

*Assassin Awakens*

*Breached: A Mystic Assassin Novella*

*Other Books from Crystal Star Publishing*

**Theresa Crater**

Spirit Springs Paranormal Women's Fiction

*The Crone and the Stolen Orb*

Emerald City Paranormal Women's Fiction

*Murder, Mystics & Menopause*

Power Places Series

*Under the Stone Paw*

*Beneath the Hallowed Hill*

*Return of the Grail King*

*Into the City of Light*

*Power Places: The Complete Series*

*Yuletide Tales: Holiday Short Stories*

Stand-Alones

*The Star Family*

*Three Awakenings: A Spiritual Memoir*

**Louise Ryder**

*God in a Box*

*School of Hard Knocks*

-

# ACKNOWLEDGMENTS

As always, special thanks go to Stephen Mehler for his patience and encouragement. Thanks to Jeff DeMarco who did a fantastic job helping me with military structure and lingo, as well as getting my guns straight. He also did a great job editing, making excellent suggestions and also finding mistakes. Special shout out to my Advanced Reader Team for their eagle eyes and helpful suggestions. All the mistakes are mine.

www.ingramcontent.com/pod-product-compliance
Lightning Source LLC
Chambersburg PA
CBHW071441260626
47170CB00008B/2786